CATHERINE FROM GIYA

A TALE ABOUT A SEVEN-YEAR-OLD GIRL FROM A REMOTE VILLAGE, GIYA IN THE SOUTHERN PROVINCE OF SIERRA LEONE, WEST AFRICA. THE FOURTEEN AND LAST CHILD OF HER PARENTS, SHE LEFT HOME AT A TENDER AGE IN SEARCH OF A BRIGHTER FUTURE. STAYED WITH AND WORKED HARD FOR VARIOUS FAMILY MEMBERS AND FRIENDS. DESPITE THE CHALLENGES SHE WAS DETERMINED TO SUCCEED.

Acknowledgement

I would like to thank my family and especially to my husband, Richard May, for all their support in writing this book.

Author: Amie Kanneh

Table of Contents

INTRODUCTION 3

CHAPTER 1 - THE HARVEST 7

CHAPTER 2 - THE DECISION 12

CHAPTER 7 - BUSINESS AS USUAL 37

CHAPTER 8 - TROUBLE NEXT DOOR..42

CHAPTER 9 - VISIT TO THE SCHOOL 47

CHAPTER 10 - RETURNING TO THE VILLAGE 52

CHAPTER 11 - BACK IN BO 57

CHAPTER 12 - THE UNREST...62

CHAPTER 13 - BACK TO NORMALITY...66

CHAPTER 14 - THE TRIPS 71

CHAPTER 16 - BULLYING NOT ALLOWED 80

CHAPTER 17 - THE PRESIDENT'S MEDICAL SURGERY 84

CHAPTER 18 - CATHERINE'S RETURN TO THE VILLAGE 89

CHAPTER 19 - FAMILY TIME AND WEDDINGS 95

CHAPTER 20 – REVISIT THE HOSPITAL...99

CHAPTER 21 - IS THE BAD WEATHER IMPACTING CHRISTMAS?.................104

CHAPTER 22 - NEW YEAR CELEBRATIONS...110

CHAPTER 24 - IS CATHERINE STAYING IN MABANG? 122

CHAPTER 25 - NEW BEGINNING 127

CHAPTER 26 - BIRTHS AND DEATHS...135

CHAPTER 27 – DEATHS AND BURIALS..141

CHAPTER 28 - WARS AND UNCERTAINTIES 148

CHAPTER 29 - TRIP TO LONDON 154

CHAPTER 30 – WEDDING, ILLNESSES AND BEREAVEMENTS........................164

CHAPTER 32 - LIFE MUST GO ON 175

CHAPTER 33 – RETURN TO LONDON 191

CHAPTER 34 - TRIP TO THE USA 201

CHAPTER 35 - BACK IN LONDON..205

2

Introduction

This is the story of Catherine, my story of Catherine, her life, her struggles, her loves. I have carried this story around with me for so long. Like an old suitcase, it has been my constant companion, wherever I have gone in my itinerant life, I have taken it with me. I now want to open that old suitcase and see what's really there, display the items for the world to see.

There is a compulsion. I must tell the story of Catherine. Catherine, is that her name? Who is she? I can hardly remember. She is a phantom. She is a ghost from my past but a presence still.

Catherine is me, Catherine is my sister, Catherine is my cousin, my mother, that tall girl I admired so much in secondary school in Freetown. Catherine is the girl I saw running to catch the bus in Bo so many years ago, oh so long ago I can hardly recall the image. It is like a photo. Is it a photo? Catherine is ....

Now what is there? The images fade, sepia fade. My life has reduced itself to this, a wide bed at the top of a Victorian house. I spend my days here, drifting in and out of sleep, keeping pain at bay, remembering, imagining the past, surrounded by photos and half-finished letters and scraps, watching the clouds scudding across the London sky, through the large velux window in the roof. I would love to jump on one and follow them to where they have been sent across the picture-frame window that lifts my mood but often the palette is dark and unmoving, unchanging for days. I welcome the storm when it comes, the tikker takker not heavy as at home but a light percussion, sending me asleep and then waking me up. I follow the patterns as the droplets.

3

But this morning I woke at dawn, half past five, run down the park and there is not a single cloud in the sky. The sky turns a deeper blue as the sun rises. Three quarter moon that has lit my room all night and I feel as if I am transplanted to a different age, a different continent.

****

Catherine woke up suddenly. It was a little after dawn and Caroline, her twin sister, stirred in the bed next to hers. It was a small room packed with clothes, buckets, and household goods but it's their room. They squeezed into it every evening, giggling and chatting away, twins who share their every thought and feeling. They were the babies of the brood of fourteen. Seven years old, the daughters of Martha and John.

Martha was the only daughter of the first-born brother of the Chief of Bumpeh. She was a beautiful, young woman, fair skinned with a gentle voice and pleasant laughter, but what made her remarkable were her eyes, blue eyes, startlingly blue eyes that seemed to see deep into your soul.

She never knew her father who died of an unknown illness, possibly malaria, before she was born, and nobody ever spoke of her mum except in whispers and out of Catherine's hearing. She was brought up by her uncle, Mikie, who never married but spent his time 'doing business' as he used to say, in particular, buying and leasing land and houses and buildings, often using the family's influence to acquire properties. He had acres of land farmed by the inhabitants of the town and surrounding villages. They had domestic staff, and she never wanted for anything except a mother.

John, on the other hand, didn't come from a well-off family. He was distinguished looking, tall with a very slight limp from a childhood accident and a prominent scar shaped like a crescent that half circled his right eye adding mystery and a touch of danger to his demeanour. Women liked him. He was a gentle man but restless, a man who couldn't settle to anything, roaming around far and wide. Originally from Yoni, a tiny village near Bumpeh, he was a good friend of the Chief Bono, Mikie's brother, who loved his stories about his adventures.

John often saw Martha when he visited Chief Bono at his palace but never really talked to her. He stared at her when they were playing draughts or chatting, intrigued. He noticed her blue eyes but mostly she was too far away. Martha could always feel his eyes on her. He piqued her interest, and she asked around about this dark, handsome man.

One day John said to the Chief that he would like to marry Martha. The Chief laughed and thought no more of it. But on the next visit John repeated his wish and again on the next visit, and he realized that John was serious. But it took many months before he made a decision. He held back because he wasn't sure that John was ready to settle down. Finally, he gave his consent without discussing the proposal with Martha. Mikie was not so keen because he regarded John as a wastrel and someone with no property or land.

After the wedding ceremonies which lasted for two days and were attended by hundreds of people from the area, Chief Bono gave a large piece of land in Giya, a rather remote village, some twenty miles from Bumpeh. He built a house for them, substantial with lots of rooms, empty and bare when they moved in. The furniture was donated by the Chief but over the next few years full of life, laughter and arguments as the family had children.

Two of them died, one in childbirth and one of malaria when she was four, but the others flourished and developed under the tutelage of their parents.

John was happy and did not regret the end of his life of travels and adventure. He looked back on those years as if it was not his younger self that lived that life but another person. He was still in love with Martha and despite the odd fractious disputes they live peaceably together. Martha never regretted the marriage. She found John delightful and funny and full of stories some of which she knew not to be true. She was tolerant of his idiosyncrasies but every so often had to put her foot down when his imagination got in front of reality, and he knew he had to back down. Life made sense for them.

Chapter 1 - The Harvest

It was a hot, sunny day and the harvest season was almost coming to an end in the village of Giya. Catherine and her thirteen siblings were helping their parents on the farm. Martha was preparing dinner in their tiny farmhouse, a small rickety old building next to their farmland some two miles from their home. She loved this time of year when all the work that they had put in over the last few months was coming to fruition. It was when all the family came together to help with the harvesting.

Martha was preparing the meal for the family and workers in the straw-built farmhouse. She had a piece of cotton cloth wrapped around her chest. Sweating profusely from the heat of the piercing sun, she wiped her face from time to time with a wet cloth and sang songs in Mende. Every ingredient was from the farm. The fish was caught from the nearby river. When she finished preparing the food, it was served in two large silver dishes: one for the men and the other for the women. Seven-year-old Catherine, the fourteenth and youngest child and her twin sister, Caroline, were only allocated basic chores but nothing too taxing. The two girls spent most of their time running around in the surrounding wild bushes playing games such as hide and seek. It was like a maze in there. They could run free over a large area.

At the top of the hill there was a stream that tumbled into a waterfall and then rapids. It wasn't too dangerous, and they bathed there sometimes. The water was cold, clean and reassuring. The music from the stream was calm and soothing. Further down where the bank was very low, women came in the morning and washed their clothes. Next to the stream was a well where drinking water was fetched.

The nearby village had twelve mud and straw built houses. From the nearby baobab trees, one could see monkeys, squirrels and rabbits playing and teasing the human race or so it seemed to little Catherine. The birds flocked to the trees in mesmerizing swarms. All year around, it got dark around six o'clock in the evening. There was no electricity in the village. At night, everyone sat around the fire, the older people telling stories to the children. At one end of the village was the courthouse. This was where disputes were resolved, and events held. Catherine's dad, John, was one of the elders, so he helped with decision making on issues relating to the village. Most evenings, the elders played draughts in the courthouse. They drank a locally brewed gin "Omole", made from fermented sugar and water. They ate kola and cashew nuts. During major events like weddings and child naming ceremonies, food was served to the village elders in the courthouse.

The work on the farm was tedious and time-consuming. On the last day of harvest, the farmers walked eight miles to the nearest market town to sell their goods buying meat and kerosene for their lanterns for their journey home and for their homes. Market days were very special for the young adults and children. It was an opportunity to meet other families from the surrounding villages and towns. The teenage boys flirted, and the girls laughed and pretended not to care. Many marriages sprung from these encounters. The children dressed up in their best attire and applied petroleum jelly to their faces. They used the black on the back of the cooking pots as eyeliners. They couldn't afford branded makeup, and, in any case, it was difficult to get hold of. It was always an exciting time for the children and young adults and an escape from the farm with its profusion of flies and insects.

And then there was the day for the trip to the market which was held in a town some miles from Giya. Catherine walked alongside her mum holding her right hand as she always did occasionally swinging them back and forth like soldiers marching. But she was quiet. Martha carried the bag of harvest produce on her head.

Then, all of a sudden, Catherine squeezed her mum's fingers causing discomfort. This was strange. Martha responded in a concerned voice, "What's the matter dear?" Catherine cried out what she had kept to herself for months, her dream: "I want to go to the city to read books like our cousins". Martha was astonished. What had brought this on? Her dad, John, who was with Caroline and was carrying some of the harvest on his back, walked up to her and picked her up and said," You can go to the big city, but we will talk about this when we return home". Catherine smiled, and the party continued the long journey to the market. Her father had agreed to her request on the spur of the moment. He was impulsive and this was a big decision. But, in fact, John and Martha had discussed on several occasions sending one of their children to the city so that they could be better educated. Perhaps Catherine had overheard their conversations in the dead of the night and her dream had been borne.

The children had heard about how well the cousins were doing in the city, but it was only Catherine, young Catherine who thought 'that is what I want to do, that is my future'. It became a secret obsession. It was an obsession borne of a visit to Bo, the regional city, when Martha took the twins to visit her cousin Maria when she was admitted to hospital and had an operation on her knee. They had stayed a few nights with Maria's family and Catherine was intrigued and motivated by the children studying and talking about becoming lawyers and doctors. She had never owned or read a book and that made her sad. She wanted the same opportunities as her cousins.

The journey to the market town took longer than expected. They walked through several villages and had to stop and greet the inhabitants as well as report to the chief of each village to register their presence. The crossing of the stream to the market town was very challenging. The makeshift bridge was wobbly and unstable, and Catherine fell in the water and got terribly soaked. She was full of laughter, though. It was an adventure. Her mum quickly took off the wet clothes and gave her clean ones from her handbag. Martha always carried spare clothing for the twins.

On arrival, all the main stalls were already set up. The traders were already trading, and buyers were haggling over goods. It was quite noisy and argumentative but good natured, but everyone wanted to sell off their harvest. Catherine's family was greeted warmly by other traders. They quickly set up their stall and began trading immediately. The older children assisted with the selling of the goods.

The twins joined the other children of similar age in the playground. The market authorities had built a play area for the children to run around while the parents traded without being disturbed. In the play area, Catherine was telling the other children that she would be going to the city to learn to read and write.   And, that she wanted to change the lives of her family when she grew older.

Caroline, her twin sister, was surprised by the turn of events and a little jealous of her sister but deep down was not that interested in moving to the city as she liked the village lifestyle. She wanted to do business and get a husband like her elder siblings who were already married but worked on the family farm, living in the same house.

After five hours of trading, the farmers sold the remaining items at a discount and, also, in exchange for items that they needed. Catherine's parents got fuel for the lantern and bought a couple of chickens that were going at knock down prices. They traded all their seeds and vegetables. They thanked each other for a successful day and went home. Catherine was a bit sad because she was not going to see her market friends for a very long time. But she knew her dad would let her go to the big city to fulfil her dreams. He would not go back on his agreement.

The journey home was much quicker than the outward journey since they were carrying less. Catherine went up to her dad and hugged him. John was a bit surprised as he knew that his daughter really wanted to go to the city. He was immensely proud of his daughter but sad that soon she would no longer be part of his everyday life. His little Catherine already had a dream at her tender age. He quickly wiped away the tears that were about to run down his cheeks. He did not want to show his emotions in front of his children. As the head of the family, he should not be seen to be weak.   He told Catherine that the family would discuss the plan the following day as they were all exhausted from today's event.

Chapter 2 - The Decision

The family had an early night after the arduous journey to the market town. Martha's feet were swollen the following morning. She noticed it when she was scrubbing her legs with a flannel. She grunted a few words in disbelief. In the village, the family used plastic buckets and cups during baths. They did not have the luxury of showers and bathtubs, but this suited them well enough as they were accustomed to that way of life. Most people went to the stream in the afternoon.

Catherine had a restless night. She did not sleep very well. She spent the night fidgeting in bed and thinking about her new life and how she was going to be successful. She would come back home to the village to build better roads and concrete houses. She would build schools and install electricity in her beloved village. All her friends would learn to read and write just like other children in the big cities.

At six in the morning, Catherine ran to her parents' room. She knocked at the door, but no one answered or came to the door. She pushed the door open and found John still sleeping. He was actually snoring really loudly. Catherine giggled because he had always refused to acknowledge that he snored. She was amused by the sound and how peaceful her dad seemed to be underneath the crocodile print sheet, without a care in the world. She jumped in and lay down next to him. She hugged him and touched his cold face. She could feel his warm breath on her face. He sneezed, and the snoring stopped suddenly. He opened his eyes and gazed at his daughter. "Did you sleep in our bed?", John asked curiously. "Is this a dream?"

This was the first time for a long time that she had crept into her parents' bed when he was asleep. Catherine nodded and said in a sweet and calm voice: "Dad, we need to talk about my trip to the big city. You promised to revisit my request today." John felt pressured. It was not an easy decision to make. Although he was excited initially about the thought of his little princess wanting to go to the city, he felt sad at the thought of not seeing her grow up. Although he knew the family Catherine was going to stay with, she was still his little baby. Maria, who lived in Bo town, had once expressed her interest in bringing up the twins when she visited the village the previous year. It would not be difficult to talk to her about Catherine's moving in with her and her family.

John got up and walked to the bathroom. He quickly splashed some cold water on his face and then brushed his teeth briskly. Martha had already prepared him breakfast, his favourite dish. It was boiled potatoes, plantains with fish stew. As he was about to sit down, Catherine ran towards the dining table and sat next to him. The three-legged wooden table was inherited from John's parents. This piece of furniture had been passed down through three generations. It was originally owned by John's great-grandmother, Sarah. It was an antique. John used a wooden bench to keep it stable. Catherine ate breakfast with her dad. This was one of her favourite moments. Everyone knew that she was very much loved by John. Her siblings called her dad's little princess. It was very quiet around the dining table. Children were not allowed to talk while eating. It was considered disrespectful. They enjoyed the meal in silence. Martha was a great cook and oversaw food preparation for major events in the village and its surroundings. After breakfast, she cleared the table, washed the dishes and put them away. The other children had already eaten and were chatting in the kitchen. Caroline was outside on the swing.

The day after every market town visit was usually relaxing. The village people stayed at home to recover from the journey and the excitement. But there was to be a party in the evening, the end of harvest party to celebrate and give thanks for the harvest and the money it had brought in. It had been a good year. Prices had remained high and there was enough money to last for months.

The food and drinks committee was responsible for the end of the harvest party. And Martha as chair of the committee had been busy for weeks organising and preparing for the party. In the evening, everyone put on their party clothes and shoes to celebrate the success of the year's harvest. The event normally took place around the courthouse. People travelled from afar to come to this event. They came with gifts for the host village. The food, alcohol, drumming, music, and dancing were the main attractions.

Before the party, John summoned a family meeting. This was scheduled to start at three in the afternoon. He invited the other elders from the village to attend. It was a serious matter. His seven-year-old daughter was about to leave the village for greener pastures. She was going to stay with Maria in Bo.

Everyone gathered in the courthouse at two thirty and the meeting was called to order at three pm to advise on the matter. After a lengthy deliberation and voting, a decision was made that she would go and live with Maria for one year. If she liked it there, then she could stay longer. The purpose was to go to school and get a job thereafter.

Catherine was so excited about the news. She ran up to her twin sister, Caroline, and hugged her. They both burst into tears. She asked her sister to come with her to Bo, but she declined. Caroline did not like Aunt Maria's children very much. They behaved differently from their village friends. They thought they were better than other children from poor families. The meeting came to an end. John thanked everyone for coming along. Martha was entrusted with the journey to the city. She had mixed feelings about her daughter's departure. She hoped that she would be happy and comfortable in her new home. The crowd dispersed and everyone went home to get ready for the evening party.

At six pm the village was full of the sound of rhythmic pulse of drums and loud music. Food and drinks were being served. The children were playing a game called "A Die" and some were using skipping ropes at the far end of the village square. It was an evening full of activities. Catherine's city news was being discussed among the older people. Some of the party guests thought the idea of sending children away was a bad one. Evil things happened in the city. They considered such places as dangerous, packed with criminals and unpleasant people.

Catherine went up to her dad to talk to him about the things she needed for the journey. John was talking to the chief from the nearby village. They did not want to be disturbed. They were talking about village issues - how to improve the area and the surrounding villages. Catherine sat quietly next to her dad. She listened to their conversation with interest. She was not allowed to contribute to adult conversation, so she kept quiet. The chief got interrupted by another elder, so Catherine took the opportunity to talk to John. "Dad, I would like you to buy a beautiful gold necklace and earrings for my trip to the big city." The children put on nice jewellery to events. Maria's children had beautiful gold necklaces. She saw them when Martha took them to see Maria. Catherine asked, "Dad, would you get me some?" With pleasure, my princess, he replied. She joined the other children who were standing around the drummers next to the courthouse. They were all dancing to one of their favourite songs.

The children went to bed at midnight. The party went on throughout the night. It was exciting for the young adults. In the early hours of the morning, some of the guests from the neighbouring villages were seen sleeping on the floor of the courthouse. They had drunk gallons of the local gin and palm wine.

Chapter 3 - The Day After

It was dawn and Catherine lay in bed listening to the birds fly past her bedroom window. She looked out. The sky was a warm azure and wispy cirrus clouds skidded across its surface. The birds were singing so beautifully this morning, celebrating my news, she thought, and maybe saying goodbye to me. "Oh, my lovely angels". These birds won't come to the city nor her half tame parrot that sometimes repeats her words. "Pretty Catherine, pretty Catherine." She would miss them, but she had so much to look forward to.

Her mum, Martha, walked into the bedroom and opened the windows wide. You need some fresh air, Martha murmured. She tied the curtains in knots to let in more light. Catherine was not best pleased as she did not like her window opened in the morning. It was freezing. "Why did you do that, mum?" Catherine asked. Martha was shocked by the tone of her voice and hurried out of the room without saying a word. The heat was on. Usually, Martha was normally a happy and free-spirited person, but the thought of Catherine's moving to the city was taking a toll on her. She had concerns. How would she adapt to a new household? How would she get along with her cousins? How would she cope with school? She had her worries, but she could see that it would be good for the family if Catherine succeeded in the future.

The village was very quiet that morning. It was time to recover from the previous days' activities. Everyone was relaxing after all the excitement. The women prepared breakfast for the visitors and their families. It was going to be another day of feasting and fun but without the noisy drums and loud music.

An hour later, the palm wine tapers arrived with fresh palm wine from the farm. It had a sweet-sour taste. They took them to the elders who had already started eating breakfast in the courthouse. Breakfast comprised boiled cassava and chicken and goat pepper soup. This was the best meal of the day and helped them recover quickly from their hangovers. Catherine's dad, John, only drank palm wine. He never smoked cigarettes or sniffed tobacco like the others. They enjoyed the breakfast a lot, finishing it all up and asking for more. The ladies and young adults also drank palm wine but in smaller quantities. It was a day of reflection and laughter. The farmers had worked hard all year, so they felt that they deserved a break and a rest. After eating, they played draughts. The young people took the dirty dishes and cutlery to the kitchen and washed them thoroughly in hot soapy water.

In the afternoon, the women and children went to the nearby river to catch some fish for the evening meal. It was a bright and sunny day. Catherine carried a miniature bucket, a spade and a fish net. She sat on the riverbank playing while Martha joined the other women fishing in the river. They caught a few more fish compared to the men's catch the previous week. They were so proud of themselves. One lady shouted, "Girls' Power!" They all shouted in unison "Girls' Power!".

The men and boys were responsible for fishing and hunting in the village whilst the women and girls were responsible for household chores, work around the farm and care for the children. The women left the riverbank after sorting out the catch and went back to the village to prepare the evening meal.

On arrival, they were astonished to find the men arguing bitterly. The atmosphere was tense, and John was being held down by two men. He was shouting at them to release him. He had drunk too much palm wine and was refusing to go home to sleep it off. Martha ran up to her husband and spoke to him in a calm but assertive voice. "John, it's time to go home." He was trying to say something to his wife, but his words were slurred and incoherent. Martha asked the two men to let go of his hands, which they did reluctantly. John tried to get up by himself, but he was too intoxicated and stumbled and fell over. He sat on the floor and Martha gave him some lemon drink. He drank some and spilled the rest on his clothes. John got up to go home but was still unstable on his feet and needed help to walk.

Catherine was upset when she saw her dad. She called her older sister, Nancy, to help their mum take dad home. When they got home, Martha gave her husband some pepper soup and encouraged him to drink lots of water and get some rest. After eating, he got up without help and went to bed. He fell asleep and started snoring. After a few hours of sleep, John woke up and was groggy but recovered. He could not remember how he had got home from the courthouse. He remembered drinking three small cups of palm wine. He had a terrible headache the previous night and had taken four headache relief tablets he bought from a trader at the market a couple of days ago, before he drank the palm wine. Martha explained what had happened at the courthouse. He had reacted to the medication. He was not meant to drink alcohol for forty-eight hours after taking the tablets. He had not read the instructions and side effects on the package. He had not read the instructions because he couldn't read. No one could read in his family.

The women returned to the kitchen to help with the preparation of the evening meal. Martha had already instructed her team on how to cook the fish. She was very concerned about her husband, so she spent most of her time checking on him. Everything was going as planned. Dinner was going to be served at eight o'clock. The communal table was set up in front of the courthouse. Chairs, benches and sleeping mats were brought out of people's homes and put around the village square. Everyone in the village and guests were present at the meal. Most of the guests from the previous evening had gone home. The food and drinks were served by some of the members of the food committee. The elderly and young men were served first, then the children. Women and young girls only ate when everyone else was comfortable and eating.

After dinner, the dirty pots and dishes were taken away and washed. The evening was very pleasant. It was a full moon, and the white light bathed the scene. Catherine and her sister Caroline were chatting about her trip to Bo. The children asked many questions about the cities and big towns. Some of them had never left the area except for the surrounding farmland and very occasional visits to local hamlets and villages. They lived very sheltered lives.

Children were sometimes coerced into early marriages. Landowners and businessmen were allowed to marry children from the tender age of twelve. Some of the children worked as slaves for their husbands. Polygamy was a popular practice. Catherine was going away from that. She would decide her own future.

It was getting very late and some of the people had already gone home. Martha and the children were fast asleep in bed when John woke them up. He shouted, "the farmhouse is on fire". Some boys from the neighbouring village had set fire to some of the farm buildings and then disappeared into the surrounding bushes. Some of the young men in the village put out the fire immediately with blankets, water cannons, hose pipes and buckets. They were well-trained. Forest fires were frequent and becoming more dangerous for the people of Giya and the surrounding villages. The extreme heat during the dry season was a contributing factor. After the fire incident, the crowd dispersed.

Chapter 4 - The Response

Earlier that day, John had asked one of his nephews, Brima, to travel to Bo to inform Maria that Catherine would like to come and live with them. Brima had walked five miles to a nearby village and rented a bicycle to the bus station. The bus was about to leave when he arrived. He beckoned the driver to wait for him. He got off and chained the bicycle to a rail and then jumped on the bus.

The six-hour bus journey to Bo was long and tedious and tiring. The roads were bumpy and dusty. There were road works everywhere, some official, with men in blue overalls hard at work and, some unofficial, with young men filling in holes and demanding money.

Construction work had just begun on the main road from Bumpeh town, where Brima had caught the bus to Bo. The traffic was horrible. The driver was good, unlike some on that route, waving to the workers and driving carefully past them. There was a brief stop on the bridge to pick up waiting passengers. A lady with four children boarded the bus. One of the children was crying. They walked along the aisle of the bus and sat in the back seat. The lady carried the crying toddler on her lap and started breast-feeding him. The crying stopped. The driver sighed. The only noise they could hear now was high-pitched sounds from the boy after every feed. The other children sat quietly. They were well-behaved.

The next stop was a petrol station. The petrol tank was filled up, and the driver paid the cashier. Some passengers got off to use the toilets, stretch their legs and buy food from the street hawkers. The small shop in the station sold drinks and other food items. Brima bought a bottle of Fanta and a packet of custard cream biscuits. The exterior of the bus was already covered in dust. The smell of petrol from the exhaust pipe was overpowering. The journey took a bit longer than scheduled because of roadblocks and traffic.

On arrival at the bus station in Bo, Brima and the other passengers got off the bus. He picked up his travel bag and walked over to the taxi rank and asked the driver to take him to Pessima Street. Maria was cooking dinner in the kitchen and the children were watching television in the sitting room when he arrived. Her husband was out of town on a business trip to Guinea- Conakry.

Brima knocked on the door and waited patiently for someone to come and open it. Maria heard the knock and went through the back door to see who was there. She was not expecting any visitors on that day. When she saw Brima, she thought something terrible had happened in the village, and he was there to convey bad news. She asked without wasting any time, "Is everyone alright?" He smiled and said yes. He was a very polite young man.

He told Maria that he had been on the road all day so some water and food would be very much appreciated. He assured her that it was good news. They went into the sitting room and when the children saw him, they ran up to him and asked, "Brima, what brings you to the city?" He couldn't wait any longer, so he said cousin Catherine would like to come and stay with you in Bo, so she can attend school. The expression on their faces was encouraging. Then Maria said, "great news!" Catherine would not marry a farmer. Maria detested children marrying at an early age.

They all sat down to a sumptuous dinner and then had an early night. Maria and her family were delighted about the addition to their family. The children were more excited about having their little cousin come to stay with them. It was then decided that Catherine would share the ensuite bedroom with her cousins. The two younger children would sleep on the bunk bed and the older sibling on the single bed. Catherine's cousins, Alice, ten and, Cecilia, eight, had never visited the village. They have only heard stories from their parents.

Brima had to catch the midnight bus back to the village. He slept for a couple of hours in the guesthouse and Maria later drove him to the bus station. After saying goodbye, he got on the bus and quickly settled in. He slept for much of the bus ride apart from the times the mosquitoes bit him. At the end of the bus journey, he picked up his bicycle and rode to Bumpeh and handed it to the hiring officer. He walked the rest of the five miles journey back to the village.

The following morning, Brima was back in the village. His trip to Bo was a success. Everyone was waiting for news from Maria. Catherine ran up to Brima as he approached the house. "Was my request honoured" she asked? "Yes, with pleasure," he replied. The family saw how excited Catherine was, so they concluded that it was all positive. Martha and John decided on a date for the trip. Martha and the twins would make the journey to Bo in a couple of days' time. Caroline was going to see her sister off. They enjoyed travelling together.

After breakfast, the family went to the farm to do some burning of the bushes and tidying up. The reconstruction of the farmhouse had begun. The fire incident had badly damaged it. Catherine and Caroline were seen carrying bundles of sticks on their heads. Nancy, the elder sister, was walking behind with a huge cutlass. As they walked along the narrow path, a large brown snake suddenly crawled over Nancy's feet and to the other side of the path into the bushes. She was shocked and frightened. She stood still for a while but was sweating profusely. Her heart was pounding so hard. Despite being accustomed to such occurrences; it was always a difficult and unpleasant encounter. The snake slithered away. She then shouted, snake!

The girls were so frightened, they immediately fled the scene, but then returned slightly embarrassed. Nancy then summoned up courage and ran in the direction of the snake and killed it with the cutlass she was carrying. Catherine was astonished because that was the first time she had witnessed the killing of a snake. The girls walked back to the farmhouse and told the others. The rebuilding of the farmhouse was nearly complete. It looked much better than the previous one. It was very spacious with an extra room for storage. After dinner, Martha and her girls went home. John and the boys stayed on the farm a bit longer to finish their drinks.

At home, Martha sorted out Catherine's clothes, shoes, jewellery and body oils for the journey to Bo. She had already packed one suitcase full and was putting together foodstuffs in the second case. She kept a small bag for Caroline and her clothes. They were going to spend a week in Bo to see Catherine settle in with her new family before returning to the village. When she had finished packing, she stored the cases in one corner of the room. Martha and the girls went outside to join the neighbours around the fireplace. Roasted peanuts, boiled corn and hot milky cocoa drinks were served. The neighbour, an older woman, Neneh told stories and funny jokes to the children.

John had joined the elders in the courthouse when they returned from the farm. The men were already planning Christmas, a week-long event. On the days leading to the twenty-fifth of December, people from the surrounding villages would come together to celebrate. Every year, they brought and shared food and drinks with the others in the village square. Catherine's village, Giya, was well known for hosting major ceremonies and events. For the first time, she was going to spend Christmas away from her family and friends in the village. It was her last day with them as she left for the city the following day with Martha and Caroline. Everyone went to bed at ten o'clock, so they could get a good night's sleep ahead of the journey in the morning. Catherine fell asleep as soon as she lay down in bed. She was relaxed and ready to start her new life.

Chapter 5 - The Journey To Bo

In the morning, around five am, Martha woke up to fetch water from the village well. She got the wood fire going to heat up water in the large pot. The hot water was used for washing and for making coffee or tea for the family. She got her older children, Nancy and Mammy, who were already awake to cook breakfast for the entire family. The breakfast was made up of chicken and lamb stew on rice and fried plantains. Some of the preparation had already been done the previous night, so it did not take long to get the food ready.

Then the rest of the family woke up and had their baths. The twins dressed up in a similar tailor-made "tie and die" outfit. They looked delightful. The family ate breakfast together as they celebrated the beginning of Catherine's new life. It was a sad day for their parents, especially John. He called the two girls to his bedroom and said to Catherine, "Princess we love and are going to miss you very much". "Remember, if you're not happy during your stay in Bo, please come back to the village." He picked up his daughter and kissed her on her forehead. Caroline leaned over John with tearful eyes. Her playmate was going away. John wiped Caroline's eyes with a piece of cloth from his pocket and then cuddled her. He parted her hair by pulling the strings backwards from her face. He was very gentle with his children, not a typical strict and no-nonsense African dad. Then he got up and walked out of the room to join the other members of his family. Martha was patiently waiting for them on the veranda with the luggage. Catherine ran out, followed by her sister. She shouted, "It's time to go".

Catherine and family left the house and everyone in the village came out to bid her farewell. She was like a little princess. Everyone stood in front of their houses and sang her a beautiful goodbye song. She was not expecting that. Catherine stood in the centre of the village and shouted at the top of her lovely voice, "Thank you so much to everyone, I'm going to miss you all!"

They walked slowly along the narrow road leading to the main road where they caught a waiting taxi to take them to the bus station. The walk was long and a bit exhausting. Brima carried the suitcases in a wheelbarrow. The sun was shining brightly, and it was getting hot. Martha, Caroline and Catherine got in the taxi and greeted the taxi driver. The ride was short but very bumpy.

When they arrived in Bumpeh, they waited thirty minutes for the bus to Bo. Martha and the girls shared a homemade sandwich and freshly squeezed orange juice. It was a fun time for the children. Other passengers were also waiting. There were petty traders everywhere plying their business. They looked forward to the bus ride. When the bus arrived from Bo, it was packed full of passengers. Most of them were traders and farmers from the surrounding villages. They had been shopping, so the luggage area was completely full. It took a very long time to offload the compartments. The driver nodded at the two men standing across the station. It was like they were waiting for his call. When they came close, he instructed them to clean the entire bus and get the queuing passengers to board. After everyone had embarked, the driver shouted across to the apprentice, "time to get going, we are running very late".

As the driver sped out of the station, he accidentally hit an elderly man who had a walking aid and was trying to cross the road without looking. The driver pressed his foot so hard on the brake and the vehicle stalled. Fortunately, the impact was minimal. The old man fell down on the road. Some passengers ran to his aid. They moved him to the side of the road and sat him on the pavement with his back against a wall.

The driver told the passengers to stay on the bus. He went out and checked what his injuries were. He asked in a calm voice, "are you alright old chap, what were you doing in the middle of the road?" A doctor and his family had just arrived for lunch from a nearby restaurant. She was a well-known medical practitioner in the district. When Doctor Abbie saw the crowd, she quickly parked her car in the car park of the restaurant and then walked over to see what was happening. At the scene, she did all the vital checks and checked for external injuries. She suggested the man be taken to hospital for further investigation just in case there were internal injuries. After a careful examination, the doctor said to the driver that there were no immediate concerns.

The bus driver, who was only recently taken on by the company and was afraid that such an incident might jeopardise his employment. He thanked the doctor and then gave some money to the old man for his expenses. He was carried over on a stretcher to an arriving ambulance and handed over to the paramedics. They were briefed by Doctor Abbie and then the patient was taken to the local district hospital in Bumpeh.

At the hospital, he was examined by Doctor Imani. A head and chest scans were requested. After several hours, the results came back. The doctor then requested a twenty-four-hour bed rest and plenty of fluid to recuperate from the shock. The nurse brought the patient a warm cup of tea and a piece of toast. The old man thanked the nurse. After drinking the tea, he slept and woke up when the doctor was doing his routine check. The old man had recently buried his wife, who suffered a sudden heart attack when they were on the farm. She had been a decent and hardworking woman and he felt alone in the world without her. He had no other relatives close by, so he stayed the night in the hospital and went home the following day.

The bus driver drove carefully along the busy and bumpy roads to Bo. Throughout the journey he had flashbacks about the accident. If he had not been more attentive, he would have killed the old man. But he remembered that he was driving too fast out of the garage in an attempt to make up on lost time. Anyway, the prognosis was not bad. He would recover from the shock and then go home.

Chapter 6 - Welcoming Party

Maria had been waiting patiently for an hour for her relatives at the bus station. The bus was delayed due to the incident in Bumpeh and the ensuing traffic. Martha and the girls were excited. Catherine called out, "Aunt Maria, you're here?" The girls ran up and greeted her. They jumped up and down and pulled her hands with gratitude.

Maria bent over and kissed the girls, turned around and said, "Hello big sister Martha, beautiful as always, how are you doing?". Martha blushed, and responded, "everyone is doing fine, thank you so much for coming to meet us". Maria chuckled and replied, "I have waited for this moment for a very long time, you have been a mother to the whole family, and I would like to help your children if you allow me". She continued, "Alice and Cecilia were delighted and couldn't wait to see you".

The drive to Maria's home took twenty minutes as she went along a different route. She stopped at the supermarket in the town centre to get some more groceries. On their way home, she took them to see an elderly lady in her nineties who had been Maria's closest friend and mentor. Madam Clarissa, commonly known as "mammy queen" was one of Bo's finest ladies. A seventy-year-old, beautiful and kind-hearted person with a heart of gold. She was married to the mayor of the city. Her husband went off with a younger woman and left her with four houses. They had six grown up children and were all doing well in society. She had brought up many children during her active years and had helped so many young people during their youth and struggling years. She had a real estate business which did very well in the past. Maria checked on her at least three times a week.

When they arrived home, Maria's girls were in the play area on the swings. There were young people cleaning and laying out plastic chairs and trestle tables in the compound. Maria's friends and neighbours were in the kitchen cooking various West African dishes; salads, jollof rice, cassava leaves, brown rice, foo-foo made from fermented cassava root, bitter leaves soup and many more. The compound was beautifully decorated with bounties, fresh flowers, colourful lights and balloons. There was a welcoming message for Catherine prepared by Alice and Cecilia. "Welcome Catherine!" it proclaimed with three red heart-shaped stickers at the entrance to the house. Martha and her children couldn't believe all the fuss that was being made of them. It was the prettiest decorations that they had ever seen. Caroline and Catherine, the twins, wandered around in disbelief. They asked Maria, "What are the celebrations for?" They ran up to their cousins in the play area and exchanged greetings. Maria's girls went up to Martha and said, "Hello Aunt Martha". She pulled the two girls up to her and embraced them tightly. "You have grown up my not so little ones."

They all went into the house where Maria's husband, Joe, was drinking with his business partners and associates. There were bottles of whisky, brandy and vodka on the table. The bottle of brandy was nearly finished. It was a glorious day. They were discussing business-related matters and politics.

The background music was soothing and very relaxing. Life seemed very different here compared to the village. The house had a luxurious look and feel to it. The air conditioning was on. It felt cold in the room. Joe stood up when he saw Martha and the twins. He said, "good to see you and the girls". He turned to Catherine and told her that she was welcome to stay as long as she wanted. Martha, Caroline and Catherine thanked him. Tears were pouring down Martha's face. She quickly wiped her eyes with the back of her hands. The tears came from nowhere. She visualized her daughter one day in high places. Catherine held on to her mum's left hand and said to her, "don't cry mum". Joe looked away and quickly sat down and continued his conversation with his business associates and friends.

Catherine's luggage was taken to their bedroom by her cousin Alice. Martha and Caroline were taken to the guest house. It was a comfortable three-bedroom house next to the main house. It had a large television and gorgeous leather sofas in the seating room. The rooms were warm and cosy. The suitcase filled with foodstuffs from the village was presented to Maria as a gift from Catherine's family.

Maria had gone to the clothing stores in the morning before picking them up from the bus terminals to buy dresses for Martha and the twins for the dinner party. When she arrived at the store, she was recognized by the salespeople. She had been a regular customer for many years. A young customer service lady walked up to her and asked, "Madam, how can I help?", "What's the occasion?" Maria replied, "Please help me find two special occasion dresses for two five-year-old girls and one for an adult, size fourteen". They looked through a few clothes rails in the children's section and found two identical mini dresses that would suit the twins very well. It was easy to find a dress for Martha as Maria was of the same size and height. After choosing the dresses, she paid and took the items home before going to pick them up at the bus station.

Martha and the girls were given towels to take a shower. Catherine took her new dress and shoes to join her mum and Caroline in the guesthouse. Martha tied the twins' hair in very nice pink and white ribbons to match their pink dresses. They looked amazingly pretty. After dressing up in their new attire, they were ushered by Cecilia into the dining table in the main house. Light food and hot cocoa drinks were served to them.

The organization was going on outside the main house. The women were finishing the preparation of the food in the exterior kitchen. The tables were laid out with pretty, floral tablecloths on which there were napkins and cutlery. It was a welcoming party for Catherine! Maria announced to her guests. She had quickly put together an elaborate soirée for her dear niece to mark the start of a new beginning.

The party guests were fifty prominent people in the community and their families. Alice's and Cecilia's friends were also invited to the party. Maria was very much loved by her friends and work colleagues, so they were always happy to help whenever she asked them. Her husband, Joe, was once a member of Parliament. Maria and her family were magnificently dressed up. They were representative of the "nouveau riche" of Bo town. Even with their wealth, they were very modest in their behaviour. They treated everyone with respect.

The party guests started arriving at seven in the evening. On arrival, they were served with drinks and nibbles by the waiters. They mingled; the conversation was loud and noisy. They could hardly hear themselves. Men gathered in small groups discussing various issues, from politics to the next business projects and ideas. The women drank wine, baileys, and fruit juice. Some wealthy ladies were seen showing off their expensive jewellery and talking about overseas business trips and vacations. Everyone sat down to a buffet at eight pm. The food was delicious. The conversation around the tables was interesting. The waiters were serving wine, cocktails and water with the meal. It was a very pleasant atmosphere. Later in the evening, the youths asked the DJ to play dance music. Most of the dignitaries had gone home by this time. They danced till very late into the night.

Chapter 7 - Business As Usual

Joe woke up with a terrible headache. Maria was still in bed, exhausted from the previous day's events. She found great pleasure in entertaining and bringing people together. Everyone had plenty to eat and drink at the party. The leftover food and drinks were distributed among the domestic staff. Before sunrise, the housekeepers had cleaned and tidied up the entire house and compound. The air smelled fresh.

Breakfast was laid out in the dining room for the family. Catherine and her cousins were out in the garden lifting up rocks and watching the beetles scurrying away. Caroline laid down in the garden hammock with her eyes closed. She was thinking about her dad in the village. Already she missed him a lot. To allay her feelings of loss, she got up and wandered around the garden. It was huge with a massive fishpond and beautiful palm trees. The gardener was in the vegetable garden at the far end digging out sweet potatoes and putting them in a basket. The decorations had all been taken down. It was like a normal day at Maria's. Martha was still sleeping in the guesthouse.

Joe's driver had arrived in the morning to take him to his meeting. While waiting, he washed the car inside out. Joe, in a dark suit, blue shirt and a pair of black suede shoes, after breakfast, kissed his wife on the forehead and walked to his car. He was meeting investors from China at a nearby hotel regarding a recently won bid on a government project. The project proposal had a fundraising aspect to it, and he was also in charge. He had to look for extra funding for the project to build a railway line in the southern region. A massive project. The government had offered the project to Joe, who had an engineering background and had a lot of international connections developed during his years in business and politics. He imported construction tools from Europe and mainland China.

Joe called out to his driver who was sitting at the security post, "Take me to hotel Belleview". The driver greeted his boss, ran up to him then took his briefcase to put in the boot of the car. He opened the door of the back seat and Joe got in. He sat down and straightened his coat and gazed at the driver's mirror. On arriving at the hotel, five men were waiting in the lobby to meet Joe. They shook hands and were quickly ushered to an air-conditioned room that was pre-booked for the meeting. They were served tea and coffee and coconut flavoured shortcakes. The deliberations were relatively short and agreeable since most of the groundwork had already been completed in the preceding weeks. The contract was signed and sealed. It was decided that work would commence the following year on the railway line. The investors would donate five trains in exchange for mining coal. Joe was very excited about the outcome of the meeting. They scheduled another meeting in six months. Date to be confirmed. He thanked the investors for their support and time. His driver was waiting in the car. As Joe approached the exit, his driver was waiting to let him in. They drove to his office.

Catherine went to see Martha in the guest room. She had woken up and sat down quietly on a stool in the veranda. She was lost in her thoughts. "Mum, are you alright?", Catherine asked. "Yes, my love." "I was just thinking about your dad, the family, and the farm. We have a lot to do this year", she continued. "The village is not going to be the same without you."

Maria, Alice, Cecilia and Caroline were watching the news on television when the phone rang. Cecilia answered. She exclaimed, it's daddy! He would like to talk to you, mum. She handed the phone to Maria. She loved her husband so much and even blushed when speaking to him.

With the phone in Maria's hands, she asked, "Daddy, I hope your meeting went well? Are you coming home for lunch?" Joe sighed and said no honey, I had lunch with the investors at the hotel. He continued, "Would you like the driver to take the children to the cinema?" "Yes, sure. I'll get everyone ready in an hour. Martha and I will come with the girls," replied Maria. "Goodbye my love and thank you!" He hung up and continued his work in the office. When he finished what he was doing, he called a taxi firm to send a car to take him to the cinema.

Joe's driver arrived in a more spacious car as expected at the house. Everyone was excited, especially Catherine. She was imagining how her new life was going to be in the city. Here she was going to the cinema. It was so exciting. They all got in the car with Maria in the passenger seat next to the driver. Before she put on her seat belt, she ensured that all the other occupants of the car had seat belts on and that they were comfortable.

She nodded for the driver to go. When they arrived at the Capitol cinema, Joe was waiting for his family at the bar. He wanted to surprise them. He had bought the tickets. They were going to see a popular Indian film suitable for youngsters. It was about a young girl who had travelled miles from the rural south to Delhi to look for work. During her struggling years, she met her husband, a wealthy prince. His parents did not accept the lowly bred girl initially because of her background. She had had a deprived childhood. In the city, she worked relentlessly to achieve her dream of becoming a plastic surgeon. One of the best in the world and her clients were wealthy people. Because of her hard work and subsequent achievements, her husband's family accepted her. Some of the story resonated with Catherine.

When Maria saw Joe she was pleasantly surprised because she was not expecting her husband at the cinema. She smiled and walked up to him, then kissed him on his forehead. He hugged her, and then they joined the others who were waiting to be directed.

"Studio six, down the corridor, turn right and then up the stairs, the first door on your right," said a cinema staff member. It was as if he had repeated those lines many times. Joe thanked him and led the group to studio six. The adverts were already showing on the screen when they entered the studio. A young lady in a security uniform checked the validity and seat numbers on the tickets with a torch and ushered them to their respective seats. The adults sat together, letting the girls share two medium-sized boxes of popcorn and small packs of Vimto drinks with straws. The adverts went on for ten minutes. As the lights were dimmed, a recorded male voice announced the duration of the film and pleaded with everyone not to speak during the film. At the end of the announcement, the voice thanked the audience for their time and was silent. The audience was so quiet you could hear a pin drop.

The film went on for two hours forty-five minutes, and then they got up and walked slowly behind a long queue of people exiting the studio. The girls went straight to the toilet to wash their hands.

Martha's eyes were red and a bit swollen. She had been tearful while watching the film.

At home, dinner was shrimp pepper soup for starters, grilled fish, roasted potatoes, salads and gravy as the main dish. Carrot cake was served for dessert. They watched a bit of television afterwards and went to bed.

Chapter 8 - Trouble Next Door

It was around four in the morning. The neighbour's dogs were barking loudly. Something was up - maybe intruders. Catherine called Alice but she was still sleeping. She got out of bed and went to the bathroom. On her way back she decided to see what was going on outside. She lifted the corner of the window curtain and saw two hooded men getting away in a truck. The dogs were still barking savagely and pulling on their lead. The continuous roaring sound was like they were crying for attention from the neighbours. Something bad was happening to their owners.

Catherine tiptoed quietly over to Alice's bed, speaking in a low voice. "Wake up, wake up! Something bad is going on next door." The girls sat up and watched through the lace curtain in the direction of the neighbour's house. A police van suddenly stopped in front of the house. Plain clothes men with guns jumped out of a van and ran towards the house. One of them pushed hard at Maria's gate. The security officer called out, "who are you, and what do you want? ". The men shouted, "open the gate! we need information about next door".

Then two loud gun shots were heard from outside the gate, bang, bang! Some of the men were already in the neighbour's house checking on them. Someone had sent a message to the special branch police headquarters informing them about strange activities in the area. Joe and Maria's security officer, who had slept throughout the incident, said,

"I did not hear anything, what's going on?". The neighbours' dogs had stopped barking.

On hearing the loud gunshots, Joe had rushed to the door and Maria walked quickly behind her husband. Joe opened the front door and called his security officer and asked what was going on? The latter was very scared. He stammered his words. "Yes sir, some men were demanding I open the gate. There had been an incident next door." In the meantime, Catherine and Alice waited anxiously wondering whether to go out to explain what they had seen. Cecilia was still sleeping soundly. She had slept through all the noise.

Catherine ran out and said, "Uncle Joe, I saw two men getting into a truck. One of them had a knife in his hand and the other man pulled out a heavy bag and put it in the truck. They sped away in that direction." Joe was impressed with what he had heard, and thanked Catherine. He told her to go back to bed. The security officer who had informed his boss that he did not hear anything was utterly dumbfounded. How was a seven-year-old girl be able to give such a vivid account of the situation?

Joe was so disappointed with his security officer and asked him to open the gate immediately. A large crowd of people were already watching from a distance. He went outside and spoke to the plain clothes officers. Gentlemen, he called out. "What's going on?" The commanding officer, who was talking to his men, looked at Joe with suspicion. "Did you hear anything? We heard dogs barking and then gunshots. My little niece just mentioned that she saw two men speed away in a truck before your arrival." Joe continued, "are the neighbours alright?" The police officer replied that they were still investigating. "Someone was bleeding from the head, but my men are dealing with it."

Joe was in deep shock because he got on very well with the family next door. He considered them friends. "Is there anything I can help with?" Joe inquired. The commanding officer thanked him and joined his men to carry on investigating the incident. An ambulance arrived, and the wounded man was laid on a stretcher and quickly transported away. Joe went back to explain what had happened to his family, who were all gathered and anxiously waiting for news in the compound. Maria was stunned. She asked if the wife and children were alright.

In Maria's household, Martha had a terrible night. In her dream, she saw Catherine flying in the sky like an eagle high up in the sky. No one could catch her. She seemed very happy. When Martha woke up from the dream, she heard the dogs barking loudly and, subsequently, the gun shots, then the bang on the gate. Terrified of what was going on around her, she went to Caroline's room to check on her. She was asleep. She took an extra sheet and wrapped it around her daughter. She stroked her hair and left the room.

The bells from the Catholic Church were ringing from down the road. It was already six in the morning. Maria and the children decided to attend the nine o'clock mass. They got ready and ate beans on toast and oatmeal porridge for breakfast and then left in Maria's car. Martha and Joe stayed at home. Martha had converted to Islam when she married John. She prayed in her room and while in Bo went to the local mosque for the afternoon and evening prayers.

On the way out, Maria stopped outside the gate and got out of the car, leaving the children. She wanted to check on the neighbour but was stopped by a tall man with wide red eyes in a police uniform who was guarding the house. He said calmly, "sorry madam,

you cannot go in there, it's a crime scene".
Forensics was on its way. They had cordoned off
the area from the public. The police van was no
longer there. Maria went back to her car, got in
and drove off.

The church service had just started when they
arrived. The girls rushed in and sat at the back
while Maria hurriedly parked the car and joined
them. It was a very good service. The choir sang so
beautifully. Communion was served, and the priest
prayed for the children. During the welcoming
message, Catherine's name was mentioned. She
stood up with pride and thanked everyone. The
congregation sang a welcoming song and applauded
at the end.

The priest invited everyone to tea and cakes in the
church hall afterwards. In the church hall, the
associate priest led a prayer for the family attacked
this morning. They were also members of the
church. No one knew exactly what had happened.
Every other person seemed to have an
explanation. Some of the conspiracy theories
include armed robbery, political opponents, and the
like. The children were in the play area building
blocks and having milkshakes. Maria spoke to the
head teacher at the Catholic school where her
daughters went about the possibility of Catherine
being admitted to the school. They scheduled a
meeting for the following day at noon.

Joe was next door when they got home. He had
been allowed in by the policeman. The neighbour,
Joseph, had just returned from hospital and was on
the sofa taking a nap. His head was wrapped up
with a white bandage. He was a bit concussed.
The wife and three children had hidden in the
basement when they heard the violent knock on the
door. When the husband opened the door, the
thieves ran in and demanded the key to the safe.

When he refused to give them, they slapped him, and he lost his balance and fell over. They stepped all over his head and pointed a knife at him.

Maria, Martha and the girls sat in the main seating room playing ludo, a family game played with two dice. It went on for a while. When Joe walked into the house they stopped to listen to him. Joe narrated the event. It was like a three-minute action movie trailer. A very violent one, but it was real. The armed robbers got away with diamonds, expensive jewellery, five hundred million leones and several bottles of alcohol. It seemed like an inside job because they knew where everything was. They were fast and effective. It was well planned.

Chapter 9 - Visit To the School

It was a school morning. Alice and Cecilia were both up. The alarm clock rang at seven o'clock. They normally took turns using the bathroom. Cecilia went in first, she cleaned her teeth with an electric toothbrush. She liked the feel of it. Maria went in to help her wash. She dried it gently with a towel and applied baby oil and petroleum jelly on her. She combed and sectioned her hair into four and tied it nicely with black and white ribbons. Alice took a quick shower and dressed up in her blue and white uniform. Her hair was already plaited in long braids. They ate breakfast together while the driver waited in the car. When done, they picked up their lunch boxes and school bags and said goodbye to their parents. The drive to school was short. It took ten minutes in the car. They got out of the car and waved goodbye to the driver.

At home, Catherine went over to Martha and Caroline's to invite them to breakfast. Joe and Maria were already eating. They were playing a card game in bed. Caroline was laughing so hard because she was winning. They paused the game and went to join the others for breakfast. During breakfast, they discussed Catherine's education. Maria was going to take her to the Catholic school to discuss it with the headteacher.

At noon, Maria drove Catherine to St Mary's Primary School for her meeting with the school authority. It was lunchtime and the students were outside. It was a mixed school. The older girls were playing volleyball, and the younger ones played a game called "Ar Pass Ya" and snakes and ladders. The boys were playing football.

Some of Cecilia's classmates saw Maria and Catherine enter the gate. They ran up to her and called, "Auntie Maria! We heard you were coming in with little Catherine. Are you Catherine?" One of the girls asked. "Yes," with a big smile, and "who are you?" Catherine asked. She wasn't shy at all, she surprised herself. The girl shrugged her shoulders and blushed. "I'm Theresa," Cecilia's friend.

Maria walked towards the reception office when Alice saw them. Her mum embraced her warmly and kissed her on the forehead. Alice was a bit embarrassed because the boys had seen her mum kissed her. She was embarrassed and quickly moved away. She told her mum that everyone was looking at them. Maria sighed and said, "Am I not allowed to cuddle my daughter?" Alice took them to the reception office and then disappeared into her classroom.

The reception manager got up to welcome Maria and Catherine and directed them to the secretary's office. The secretary was a very polite young lady who had recently joined the school. Her smile lit up the room when they entered the office. She asked, "How can I help?" "I have a meeting with the head at twelve", Maria responded. The secretary offered them seats. I will let her know you are here. She informed the headteacher that Maria was waiting to see her. "Please let them into my office", the headteacher said.

When Maria and Catherine entered the office, the headteacher made them feel comfortable and at home. She stood up and gave Maria a firm handshake and beckoned them to sit down. Maria thanked her and sat down. She had a very serious demeanour about her. A straight face with a pair of huge, rounded glasses. "What is her level of literacy?", she asked. "None", replied Maria. The headteacher was astonished because Catherine's verbal English was very good.

After a lengthy deliberation, it was decided she would spend six months in reception with extra private tuition to help her catch up with the class. "If she exceeded expectations, then we will transfer her to the next level," the headteacher concluded. Maria thanked her for the opportunity and reiterated her family's appreciation for all the support over the years. Catherine was extremely happy and thanked the headteacher and promised she would do her best.

By the time they left the headteacher's office, the school was almost finishing for the day, so Maria decided to take Alice and Cecilia home. She phoned her husband to let him know that she would take the children home after school.

On the drive home, Maria stopped at the ice cream shop and bought ice cream for the girls. It was a bright and sunny day, and the cooling system was a bit faulty, so they were all sweating profusely. They drove to the park and sat on a long bench under a baobab tree. Maria told her girls that Catherine was going to start school the next day. The ice cream was a celebration. "Good news!", Cecilia shouted.

They spent some time in the park before going home. The girls discussed the highlights of their lessons and school activities. A young boy was bullied by some boys in the playground. He was hit on the nose and pushed to the ground. Blood spilled out of his noise. It was quite disturbing. The welfare officer dealt with it because the headteacher was in a meeting. He was treated at the sick bay by the in-house nurse. The wounded boy's parents were called to the school and the boy was taken away. Letters were sent to the three boys' parents involved in the bullying incident inviting them to an emergency meeting the following day.

Maria and the girls arrived home a bit late in the afternoon. Martha was anxiously waiting for them in the main house. The cook had prepared dinner for the family. She normally worked four days per week and Maria prepared the meal the other days. Maria liked cooking for her family when she was not busy with other matters. Sometimes she helped in Joe's business. Not too long afterwards, Joe came through the door and was greeted by his family. Maria asked, "how was your day, darling?". He looked sad. Well, good and bad he responded. Maria walked up to him and kissed his cheek. I'm so sorry, let us discuss whatever it is over dinner. Go in and freshen up while I heat up the food.

The family gathered around the dining table. Maria served the meal while Martha poured drinks in the glasses. The meal was delicious. The girls finished and excused themselves from the dining table. Joe gave the good news that the building materials and construction equipment had arrived at the shipping port. The bad news was customs sent an invoice of five hundred million leones to clear the goods. He had been on the phone all day trying to negotiate but the customs officers insisted on that amount and any further delay would generate interest on the fee. That was a hundred percent increase from what was initially anticipated. It would have a knock-on effect on other parts of the project and the railway construction project funds.

Maria was shocked when she heard the inflated amount, but she knew without her moral support and encouragement Joe would not be willing to pay and the shipment would incur interest. Joe could be stubborn, but Maria knew how to deal with this. She had had a lot of experience over the years. Joe said his company would soon commence work on the new railway line, and that they had secured donations from the Far East for the new trains and rolling stock.

Alice and Cecilia were done with their homework. They went to the bathroom to brush their teeth before going to bed. Maria gave Martha the good news about Catherine starting school the next day. She was very pleased. Martha thanked her and joined Caroline in the guesthouse. They all had an early night which they certainly needed after all the activity and celebrations of the last few days.

Chapter 10 - Returning To The Village

In the morning, the three girls got ready for school. It was Catherine's first day at school. Excited beyond words, she was the first to wake up. Martha had told her the previous night that she would get her ready for school in the morning. Martha woke up early. She went to the main house, bathed her daughter and dressed her up in a new floral dress bought by Maria. Her school uniform would be ready in a few days. She looked so pretty. She offered to help with the other children, but Maria said no need, my dear Martha. "The girls are used to her getting them ready in the morning."

They ate breakfast together and the girls stood up and picked up their schoolbags. It was time for goodbyes. Caroline hugged her twin sister and tears were running down her cheeks. She said," We love you so much. Please be a very good girl for aunt Maria and uncle Joe. I have no doubt they love you." She looked at Alice and Cecilia and said, "cousins, please be always kind to my sister." Caroline turned to Catherine and continued," Please do come visit us in the village every so often". Emotions were running high. The children waved goodbye to Martha and Caroline. Joe's driver took them to school. It was Catherine's first day at school and the start of her journey to a better life.

Martha and Caroline went to the guesthouse to get ready for their departure. Maria was going to drop them at the bus station. They packed all their belongings in suitcases and the security guard placed them in the boot of the car. Before they left, Maria took them over to see the neighbours to commiserate with them. That was the first time since the thieving incident they saw them. They spent ten minutes and left for the station.

The drive to catch the bus was awkward. Martha and Caroline were sad about leaving Catherine behind. They did not speak throughout the journey. At the station, they got off and collected their suitcases. Maria picked up Caroline and rubbed her face affectionately against hers. She told her to come visit any time. She shook hands with Martha and then hugged her, patting her on the back.

The bus to Bumpeh was already boarding. They bought the tickets from the driver who was standing at the side entrance of the bus. The driver's apprentice took the cases, labelled, and stored them in the luggage compartment. They got on and sat in their respective seats. Maria parked her car and returned to the platform. She wanted to see them depart before driving back home. When she got home, she went back to bed feeling very sad. Martha was one of her favourite relatives. Although Martha didn't say very much, she cared for Maria when they grew up together in the village.

The bus journey was slow, and as usual, bumpy. The road works were ongoing, causing heavy traffic in places. The driver stopped a few times to pick up passengers along the way. Some farmers and small shop owners were returning home from selling their products. They had been buying goods at wholesale prices from Bo and the neighbouring towns to resell to their communities. Martha recognized some of the traders.

An elegant young lady walked up to Martha and greeted her. She then sat next to her and introduced herself. She was the daughter of a shopkeeper in a nearby village next to Giya. When Caroline saw the lady, she whispered in her mum's ear. She was my brother James' girlfriend. She went to Giya several times to see him. Martha smiled and said to the lady, are you, my daughter-in-law? And what's your name? She blushed and nodded her head. 'Alice ma', she replied. "What a beautiful name", Martha said. "Please come visit us in the village." "Sure, I will come next week, Ma. Thank you!"

They had a toilet break when they arrived at the petrol station. The driver refilled his tank and some of the passengers got off to use the toilets. It was quite a noisy environment with street sellers selling their wares. Martha had boiled eggs and ham sandwiches and a bottle of water she shared with Caroline and Alice. After eating, Caroline slept on Martha's lap. They have two more hours before arriving in Bumpeh. Some passengers got off on the way and others got on.

At a checkpoint, five traffic police men were seen stopping vehicles. There was a long queue of cars. Two men waved down their bus. As soon as the driver came to an abrupt halt, the men shouted, "Open the door!". When he did. The asked for his driver's license. He looked in the side pocket of the vehicle and took out a piece of paper. The men looked at the document and gave it back to him. His documents were up to date. The traffic officers stood still looking at the driver and the passengers.

The driver asked, "is everything alright, please can I go now?". One of the men said, "It is sunny. We are thirsty. Anything for your brothers?" "Yes indeed, the sun is hot so what would you like me to do about it?", replied the driver. "We are running a bit late, so I need to get going." He took ten leones notes from his dashboard and handed them to the men. They got off the bus immediately without thanking the driver. They hand gestured to the others to allow the bus driver to proceed. The driver drove carefully passing the checkpoint and sped away. He sighed to himself at the level of corruption.

At sunset, the bus arrived in Bumpeh. The passengers got off, and their luggage was handed over to them. Martha hugged Alice and said, "Hope to see you soon'. Alice went the opposite direction to where her dad was waiting in his truck. She got in and as they drove away, she waved at Martha and Caroline.

The queue at the taxi rank was long. Several buses arrived from the big towns and cities at the same time. Martha and Caroline walked over and joined the queue. When it was their turn to get on board an old lady rushed in front of them and pushed little Caroline. Martha caught her before she could hit her head on the tarmac. She exclaimed, "Why did you push me?". The old lady ran so fast down the road. "She is mad", someone shouted from the crowd. They got into the taxi with two other people. They were all going to the same village. The other people in the taxi were very pleasant. Caroline was still in shock from the incident before they boarded the taxi. Martha carried her in her lap and kissed her on her forehead.

When they arrived at the stop before the journey to Giya, John and Brima were waiting for them. They were so excited about seeing them. Brima took the suitcases from the boot of the taxi with the help of the driver. Caroline ran up to her dad and jumped high on him. He picked her up and gazed into her eyes and turned to his wife and the three of them embraced. "Hello there," Caroline spoke in a calm voice. "Thank you for coming with dad to meet us. Hope you have not waited long." "Not at all," Brima responded. They started the long walk to the village. John asked after Catherine and the rest of Maria's family. Martha's countenance changed. "Catherine started school today. She is going to attend the same Catholic school with Maria's two daughters. They had a welcoming party on Catherine's behalf. It was a grand occasion with dignitaries from all walks of life attending. We had so much fun. Maria and Joe are decent people."

The path to Giya was narrow and a bit bushy. It was getting dark. John came with a huge torch and a kerosene lantern. The stars in the sky shone so beautifully. When they arrived at Giya, the other family members welcomed them. Nancy had cooked chicken stew and couscous with fried plantains. They freshened up and sat down to a delicious family meal around the fireplace. All of Martha's children cooked very well, apart from the twins who were a little too young as yet to have that responsibility.

During the meal, they told the family about what went on during their visit to Bo; the dinner party, the armed robbery incident with the neighbour and the bus journeys. Martha proudly told John that Catherine was a heroine because she was the only one who saw the two-armed robbers leaving the scene.

Chapter 11 - Back In Bo

The girls had just returned home from school. Maria and the house help were in the kitchen preparing the evening meal. The girls greeted everyone and were hugged by Maria. "How was your first day at school?", Maria asked Catherine. "Aunt Maria, I had a great time. During the school assembly this morning, the headteacher announced the names of the newcomers and called them up on stage." Catherine was introduced as an ambitious, sweet young girl from the village of Giya. "Also, the children in my class were very pleasant and welcoming. The teacher, Madam Boima knows my mum." Maria knew that she came from Giya. She had left the village at a young age to pursue her dream. She went to school in Freetown, the capital of Sierra Leone, and later went to Njala University to study for a degree. She graduated in biochemistry and worked in that field for several years. "That's wonderful," Maria responded. "Yes, we all grew up in the village."

The girls went to the room to change into their house attires after showering. They sat at the desks in the room and completed their homework. Alice helped Catherine revise the alphabet and numbers. By the end of the first day, she was able to read the twenty-six letters with minimal support. She was a quick learner. She was determined to make it in life. But she struggled a bit with numbers.

The family gathered around the dinner table without Joe. He was out at a business dinner that evening with his associates. Maria and the girls watched the news on television after the meal. Then came shocking news, breaking news about a failed coup d'état. The supposed perpetrators were captured and imprisoned. There was unrest in the capital city. There had been gun shots around Freetown. The government had passed a curfew from sunset to sunrise, but the provincial towns were not directly affected. The fighting was limited to the capital city. According to the plan, if they had succeeded, they would have attacked other big towns, like Bo town. The intelligence agency was very quick in resolving what would have been a disaster.

But Joe and the other party attendees were not aware of what was going on. They were busy focusing on government projects and networking. They had lots to eat and drink. It was a champagne dinner party with over fifty prominent guests.

Maria got up and went to the bedroom and gave Joe a call. The phone rang a couple of times but no response. She left a brief message. "Honey, please call me. Something serious has been going on in Freetown." Joe did not hear the phone ring because of the background noise at the dinner party.

Before he left the office after the dinner, he saw several missed calls on his phone from his wife. He immediately dialled her number and she answered. Joe asked, "are you alright?" Maria responded, "yes. Have you listened to my messages?" Joe hadn't listened to his voice messages. "Well, there was an attempted coup in the capital, but it was foiled. It would have been awful if they had succeeded. Where are you now?" Joe was shocked. He thought the days of coup attempts was over after years of relative stability. He thanked her for sharing the news and said that he was ten minutes away from home.

When Joe arrived home, Maria was waiting for him in the lounge. She was very concerned as a wife of an ex-politician. They were the first set of people that would be sought out and attacked when there was political uncertainty. The children were already in bed sleeping. He rushed out of the car and walked up to his wife. They hugged so tightly and looked into each other's eyes. "It's going to be fine." Joe said.

He phoned his friend, the chief of the armed forces, to get details of the news. His secretary answered the call and said that the boss was in a high security meeting with the president and his cabinet. She confirmed to Joe that the news was accurate.

Later that evening, the military chief returned Joe's call. They spoke at length. He said Bo had been their next target, but fortunately, some of the alleged perpetrators were on the watch list of the Secret Service, so their daily activities were being monitored. There was a leaked document a month ago, so they were secretly on high alert. "Hopefully, there will be no more of that rubbish," he continued. "What did they want?" Joe asked.

The government was working hard to get the country back on track. Things had improved immensely. The army chief said they were asking for all sorts of things, including job opportunities for every able-bodied person and free school meals, especially for the less fortunate. The president was determined to get rid of institutional corruption. The hospitals had been refurbished and new equipment installed. A new blood bank facility had been built in the east of the country. The roads were better maintained. The water systems had been upgraded and electricity was more regular in most regions. They were not sure why people were disgruntled. The two men ended the phone call, and the military chief promised to update Joe on a regular basis if there was any change. Joe thanked him and wished him well.

The girls woke up when they heard Joe on the phone. He was now sitting on the sofa in the sitting room. They went out to inquire about the situation. Joe responded that it was all fine. A small group of people were caught trying to overthrow the government, but it had been taken care of. He suddenly remembered it was

Catherine's first day at school. He asked her how it went. Excited, she said 'very good Uncle. I can read my ABC and 1,2,3. Alice helped me learn them quickly. Madam Boima, my teacher knew the family back in the village very well. She was a friend of Aunt Maria and my mum. They grew up in the village before she went to the city". "That's amazing, she's a fantastic and well-respected teacher," Joe added. He was very occupied with the news.

The children went back to the room but spent some of the evening watching the news on the television. The headline news was that the attempted coup had failed. The perpetrators have been handcuffed. Some of the men and women were injured quite badly - they had blood on their torn clothes and faces. They looked somehow very vulnerable, sad even, tired and haggard. They had been stripped of their footwear and personal belongings when they were caught.

The government was extending the curfew to Bo and other big cities and towns. Before midnight there was another report stating that some of the culprits had confessed during interrogation that some senior government officials paid them to stage it. A few prominent names were mentioned, but those men were overseas representing the country at a conference. The president had asked for their immediate return. Their homes had been searched and police officers guarded their families. The borders were closed - no one was allowed to leave the country. The airports and road checkpoints had been notified. Everyone was asked to travel with some form of identification. And then there was an announcement that a two-day curfew was imposed on the country. Offices, schools and businesses were closed. Everyone was asked to stay at home. The only people allowed on the roads were military and medical personnel. The country was in a state of alert.

The news was horridly depressing and that kept Joe and Maria awake. Joe shouted angrily, curfew for two days! He thought the worst was over because the country had gone through so much trouble in the past. He called his driver and told him to stay at home until further notice. The security guard stayed in the boys' quarter at Maria and Joe's.

Chapter 12 - The Unrest

Catherine was sad to learn in the morning that there was a curfew, and she would not be going to school. She was a bit depressed and stayed in bed all morning. Alice and Cecilia needed a break as they were feeling a bit exhausted from the lengthy hours in school, so they did not mind staying at home. They had the opportunity to spend more time with their parents because their dad was always away. He had been out of the country travelling a lot of the time and, when he was in Bo, he was occupied with various meetings at the office and around the country.

Maria went to the kitchen to prepare breakfast for the whole family. As a treat, they were going to eat Thai-style fishcakes, a smoked salmon salad and bean cake. The children had a choice of hot chocolate, fresh mango or pineapple juice. Joe had lost his appetite because of the current unrest in the country. He had a business trip to China planned for the following week. Because of the uncertainty, he did not think it would be possible.

Maria laid the table and invited everyone to sit down. It was almost eleven o'clock. She served the food, but Catherine was still upset about school. She asked when they were returning to school. She did not trust the news. Maria encouraged her to eat a bit more. Joe drank a cup of coffee and ate a piece of fishcake. He picked up a glass of water and his notepad and went to the lounge to make a call to his contact in China. He dialled the operator to put him through. A man who spoke Cantonese answered the phone. Joe requested to speak to his contact but the person at the end of the phone did not understand English. Joe repeated the request, and the line went dead. He tried several times to get through but had no response. He was told by the operator that the connection was bad, and he should try later.

A couple of hours later, his phone rang with an international caller ID. It was his business associate in China. "Hello Joe, I heard what was going on in your country". "Dirty business!" "What about your trip next week? Will you be allowed to travel out of the country?" Joe sighed and said, "I'm not sure at this stage. When things improve in the next couple of days, I will let you know. The documents and presentation for the trip are ready. If my circumstances change and things are still unsettled, you will have to present them on my behalf." "That's not a problem. Please update me with any changes." The country was in a state of emergency. The streets were very quiet apart from a few military vehicles and the siren noise from ambulances.

Catherine and her cousins were in the bedroom watching cartoons when Maria walked in. Why are you not studying? Have you done your assignments? "Not yet," replied Cecilia. Please can you switch off the television and do some schoolwork?" They took the books from their respective bags and sat at the desk. Alice responded that she did not have any homework but would read her literature textbook. She was fascinated by the Merchant of Venice. The language was difficult to understand but the story gripped her. Cecilia needed some help with her Mathematics and English language assignments. She asked her mum to check what she had done. Maria sat with her and showed her the best possible steps to achieve the answers to the questions.

Catherine practiced writing the alphabet. Initially, she struggled so hard to hold the pencil the right way. She scribbled the letters but was very determined. After several attempts, she wrote her first letters clearly. She shouted with excitement and startled everyone. Maria looked up surprised. "Are you alright Catherine?' "Yes, Aunt Maria, I've finally got it." "Got what exactly?" Maria asked. "I wrote the alphabet today." Catherine responded. "That's wonderful! You're doing very well. Keep it up!"

Joe was worried about his forthcoming trip to China and the current situation in the country. He spent the morning pacing back and forth in the living room and around the house. Like a caged bear.

He had been on the phone on and off all morning. In the afternoon, he took out his laptop to check on his business affairs. His shares on the stock markets were doing well. He made a profit of five hundred dollars on his shares over the past few days. Not all gloom, he whispered to himself. He laughed loudly. Maria walked past him and stopped. "Someone seems very pleased with themselves", she commented. "Oh yeah, the Asian stock market is doing pretty well." If it continues like that, he will invest more. Fair enough, maybe it was time for Maria to start investing in stocks.

Joe continued, "When you're ready just let me know, I will show you the tools that have worked consistently for the last twelve months". Maria sat next to her husband, and they installed the application and linked her bank details to the account. They listened to the step-by-step guide on how to use the app. She started with one hundred dollars and in less than an hour she had an increase of twenty dollars in the account. She was excited and decided to increase her capital to two hundred pounds. She was glued to the phone screen and watching the markets fluctuate. That went well for a while, and she decided on doing the chores around the house.

The country was still observing curfew. There were no movements on the roads. Bo was like a ghost town. The news had been updated, and the President went on air to make an announcement that the curfew would be lifted on day three. One could hear people rejoicing in the neighbourhood. Catherine and her cousins heard the noise and went out of their room. "Does this mean we are going to school tomorrow?" The girls asked. "Yes, indeed." Maria assured them. "Would you all go in and sort out your school bags and tidy up the beds? When done, go freshen up and dinner will be served in an hour." They nodded and went to their room. Maria went to the kitchen to continue cooking the meal. She had to do the chores all by herself. The house helpers were not in because of the unrest. Maria phoned the workers to resume work the following day after hearing the news.

At dinner, they discussed plans for the week. Joe would fly out to China for the conference at the end of the week. The driver would come to the house every morning to take the children to school and pick them up in the afternoon and drop them off at home when Joe travelled. The children helped with the washing of the dishes and dirty pots. They cleaned around the dining table and then went to watch television. At nine o'clock, the bedroom light was switched off by Alice, and they went to sleep. By the morning, the crisis appeared to be over.

Chapter 13 - Back To Normality

At five in the morning, the roads were already busy. The Muslim call to prayer was heard from the nearby mosque. It was noisy out on the streets. You could hear passers-by talking loudly about the coup and the curfew. Joe's driver had arrived an hour early waiting to take his boss to the office and the children to school. As the driver drove out of the compound, Maria ran towards the car and called out to the driver to stop the car. She walked to Joe's side of the car and whispered something in his ear. Joe immediately got out of the car and went back to the house. He instructed the driver to take the girls to school and come back to get him.

He had something important to deal with. Catherine was concerned that something was wrong. She was just a child, and she did not want to interfere in adult business, so she kept quiet and observed. Alice and Cecilia were used to their parents' reactions to news of varying types. They hoped it was nothing to do with his business ventures.

Maria handed the phone to Joe. It was the President himself. The president! Joe gasped. He quickly took the handset and said, "Hello Mr President" in a polite and calm voice. "This is an honour. How may I help, sir?" "I'm sending you a car to pick you up to take you to the airstrip at two pm. A military helicopter will be waiting for you. I need to talk to you in person about a private issue." "Yes, Mr President, I'll be ready". "Thank you!" And the phone went dead.

Joe was worried and suddenly started sweating profusely. He had an onset of migraine that bothered him when he was nervous. Maria asked him what was going on? He had a strange look on his face. He was in shock. He wondered why the President called him – it was most unusual. He kept on thinking why me? Why me? This was the first time the president had made a direct call to him. Considering the current state of affairs, everyone was terrified. Maria got him some paracetamol with a cold bottle of water. She wiped his sweat away with a wet towel. She stroked his back and assured him that it was going to be alright.

The driver had returned after dropping off the girls. When he went back for Joe, he was instructed to take the day off and resume in the morning. Maria packed a small luggage case for her husband's trip to the capital. In the case was his two smart suits, white long sleeve shirts and red silk ties. At exactly two in the afternoon, a black Mercedes with tinted windows pulled up in front of the gate. The house phone had rung twice as a sign that the car was outside. Joe, who was already dressed up in casual? clothing, got up and said goodbye to Maria. They embraced and he left. The drive to the airstrip took thirty minutes. He was ushered to the helicopter by a man in combat fatigue. The flight to Freetown took an hour. They landed in the President's compound.

In Bo, Maria had just gone to pick up the girls from school. When she arrived, the children were surprised since they were not expecting her. Cecilia and Catherine asked if everything was fine. Joe's driver had promised to take them to the ice cream shop after school. Alice was very quiet because her instinct told her that something was going on with her dad. "I'm here now," Maria told them. "Please get in the car, and we can buy some ice cream from the stores to take home."

At the store, the girls chose their favourite ice cream flavours. Catherine liked vanilla and Maria's daughters got chocolate and strawberry respectively. They got some carrot cake and a cheeseburger as well. When they got home, the girls went to the bathroom to wash, then changed into their pyjamas. They sat at the dining table and snacked on the items they bought at the stores. Maria then told the girls that Joe had to attend an urgent meeting in Freetown. "He may not be able to return home tonight", she said. Alice interrupted her by asking what the meeting was about and why the secrecy that morning. "Oh darling, it was a private telephone call, so I had to be discreet and not to excite or alarm anyone."

On arrival, Joe approached the presidential palace with a mix of trepidation and resolve. He was taken to a luxurious room with two large windows overlooking a huge rose garden. As he was about to relax on a comfortable leather sofa, an attractive looking lady entered the room to offer him a drink.

"Would you like something to drink, sir?," the lady asked. "Yes please," Joe responded, "a glass of cold water would do." "It's a very hot day" he continued nervously. She placed some ice cubes in a glass of water from the drinks cabinet and handed it to him. He gulped the water down and then asked for a refill. The security guard came in and said, "Sir, the president is ready for you. Please can you come with me?"

Joe got up and followed him. When they arrived at the entrance of a big white door, the guard announced that he was with him. A senior military officer opened the door and Joe entered the room. He greeted the president and was offered a seat. Before sitting down, they shook hands and Joe bowed as a sign of respect. "Gentlemen, you can now leave the room," the president instructed his security officers. "Yes sir!" And the officers left.

The two men were left to conduct a tete a tete. "Joe, I have not told anyone what I am about to tell you now. You have been my closest ally and confidant for more than a decade. I'm aware what I am going to ask of you is huge, but I have no doubt you're the right person for the job." Joe's curiosity was beginning to get the better of him. He interrupted, "Are you alright, Mr President?" He paused and replied, "Yes Joe, all's well. Shall we take a short tea break now?" The two men, hand in hand, walked over to the tearoom where they drank green tea and nibbled on cakes and cookies. They talked briefly about the current state of affairs.

They went back to the president's office to continue with the conversation. "Well, let's get down to business. I'm thinking of stepping down next year due to a terminal illness. I was diagnosed last month when I went for a routine medical checkup in Germany with stage four lung cancer." Joe was utterly dumbfounded by all that he had just heard. He jumped out of his chair and hugged the president, ignoring protocol. The two men embraced tightly with Joe patting him on his back. Tears streamed down his face. The atmosphere in the room was sombre. Joe offered him some water. They talked about the possibility of him travelling overseas for medical attention. He was already talking with his doctor in Germany regarding further treatment. He would like Joe to accompany him. Also, he would employ him as his personal adviser on government related matters. The plan was for him to inform his cabinet that the trip was partly business and that he needed clarification on some medical condition. They did not want to alarm the country. The trip was scheduled to take place in a couple of weeks. All the information relating to Germany would be communicated in due course.

The President called his secretary via the intercom to arrange for a car to take them to lunch. After the meal, Joe flew back home to his family. He got a taxi home from the airstrip.

Chapter 14 - The Trips

Catherine was brushing Maria's hair in the living room when Joe arrived. He was a bit relaxed after the excitement of the day. She knew her aunt had been anxious all day since she picked them up from school. Alice and Cecilia were in the bedroom watching cartoons on television. "Uncle, where have you been? Hope your trip was good." He nodded his head, kissed Catherine on her forehead and then went to see how his children were doing. "Dad!", shouted Alice and Cecilia. "You're back!" Maria and the children were very happy seeing him. She asked if everything went well. Joe gestured with his hand to his wife to join him in the bedroom.

"The president would like me to go on a business and personal trip with him to Germany in a couple of weeks. He needs a medical check as well while we were there. Also, he offered me a job as his personal adviser. If accept, I would travel on a regular basis to the capital." Maria was pleased for him, but she was not happy about the fact her husband was accepting a job when the country was in turmoil.

At the end of the week, Joe flew to China on the planned business initiative. His presentation was very impressive, and a few more investors expressed an interest in partnering with him on his projects. He also secured more rolling stock for the rail project. After the meetings, he spent an extra day sightseeing and shopping for his family. He visited manufacturers to discuss raw materials and equipment for Freetown. The following day, he flew home. The flight was long and tiring. He flew to the airport in Lungi and his driver was at the airport waiting to take him to Bo. They landed safely, and his luggage came through very quickly.

Joe was exhausted by the time he got into the car. He slept throughout the journey to Bo. When they arrived, the girls were still in school. Maria had gone to the office to check on the staff. Usually, she worked from home. Joe got into the bath for a soak with lavender oil and Himalayas bath salt added to the warm water. He laid in the tub with his eyes closed for ten minutes. He cherished peace and quiet in the house. Maria and the children got home in time for dinner. The house help had been busy cooking the meal. They went in and got ready. At the dinner table, Joe was drinking a glass of white wine. He had bags of gifts for everyone.

As the other members of the family sat down to eat, he thanked his beautiful wife for all her support. "You are my rock. A lady of virtue and a great friend." Maria blushed and asked him, "what have you done now?". He laughed, and said, "Do I have to do something to be kind to my wife?". The girls giggled upon hearing the exchange. They ate a wonderful meal and Joe told them about his trip to China. He was so excited about his presentation and the outcome. "It was a terrific conference! We had five hundred people in attendance. It was well organized. I have something small for each of you." He handed the bags to Maria and the children. They were grateful for the gifts. The girls all had similar gifts; school bags, shoes, socks and chocolates. Maria received a gold set jewellery and a bouquet of flowers. They got up, thanked him, and hugged him.

Maria had organized a spa weekend for her and the girls. Joe would stay at home to organize his next trip with the president. It would be Catherine's first spa visit. She asked what they were going to do at the weekend spa. "It is a treat, darling. It will be revealed when we get there." They got ready and packed a lunch bag. When they arrived, the spa owner welcomed them. They were in for facials, nail spa, body scrubs and massages over two days. They stayed in a comfortable double-sized room. The first day was a bit relaxing. They changed into white gowns, disposable slippers and headbands. Four therapists walked towards them with a glass of water for each client. They led Maria and the children to the treatment rooms. The rooms were filled with the smell of essential oils. They had skin rejuvenating facials. As part of the routine, their faces were exfoliated, masked and massaged. The next day, after breakfast, they went swimming in the pool before having their nails filed and painted. The massages were in the evening after a game of table tennis and volleyball and before the buffet meal. The girls had great fun.

At home, Joe had invited his business-related associates to brief them on his recent trip to China. He hinted to them that he was thinking of accepting a lucrative job working alongside the president. They were not overly surprised because he was hard-working and wanted the best for the country. He was discreet about the President's illness. He briefly mentioned his trip to Germany with the head of state in the coming week.

Maria and the girls drove back home after the retreat. They checked on the next-door neighbour. Catherine had been interested in knowing what had happened after the armed robbery. When they knocked at the door, a strange voice answered. "What do you want?" Maria responded that they were the neighbours next door. He opened the door and told them that the family had travelled to the village for a wedding ceremony. They thanked him for the information and then left.

Joe's meeting had ended, and his associates had just left before his family returned home. The driver was loading his suitcase in the car when Maria drove into the compound. The security guard greeted Maria and directed her to park her car in the space away from the exit. The girls went up to Joe and told him they had a wonderful time, but it would have been better if he had gone with them. The highlight for all three of them was the massage. It was very relaxing and after the treatment they had a restful night. Actually, they all slept soundly till morning. They thanked Maria for the experience.

Joe was about to leave for Freetown as they flew out to Germany the following day. He was travelling by road this time. He did not want to be picked up by a helicopter. He kissed his wife goodbye and waved at the girls. Catherine and Cecilia jumped on him, pulled down his t-shirt and hold his hands firmly. Cecilia said, "Dad, we hardly ever see you". "I work hard to make you comfortable. Did you like the Spa?" Joe asked. 'Yes, we did," all three of them responded. "Someone paid a lot of money for that." Joe concluded. He got in the car, and they drove off. Joe felt bad but he wanted the children to appreciate the sacrifice he was making for his family.

The roads were recently tarmacked, so they had a smooth drive. They had one stop at the main junction leading to the north, east and west of the country. Joe wanted to inspect the road works to report back to the president. He was quite impressed by the standard and quality of the job. The journey took five hours. He stayed in a hotel close to the President's resident. The driver stayed in a guesthouse down the road. Joe called the President's office to inform him that he had arrived. The flight to Germany was at noon in the head of state's private jet.

The flight took six hours from Freetown to Hamburg with a short stop for refuelling in Italy. The jet landed at a private airport quite close to the hospital. The medical team were waiting for the president's arrival. A wheelchair personnel took him to the VIP lift with Joe walking behind them. In the doctor's office, he suggested bedrest and no alcohol. A nurse came into his room to take his temperature and blood pressure and some blood for a full blood count test. A mobile scanning machine was used to scan the affected areas. Depending on the results of the scans and blood tests, he would have surgery in the morning. Joe stayed in a private lodging in the hospital building. It was an ensuite cosy room mostly rented out to families of people in high society.

Chapter 15 - School Day

The six o'clock the alarm rang in the girls' room. Alice got up and went to the bathroom. She was brushing her teeth when Catherine went in to use the loo. Alice shouted angrily, "Don't you have manners, young lady?" "I'm so sorry. I have a bad stomach. Not sure what I ate," replied Catherine. "Well, such behaviour is unacceptable in the city. Why don't you disappear back to where you hail from? Did you think we want to share our parents' wealth with a stranger?" Catherine burst into tears. Cecilia overheard the conversation and rushed to save her cousin from her sister's spiteful words. "What did she do to you?" Cecilia cried out. Catherine flushed the toilet and ran out. That was the first time she missed her family back in the village. Alice showed no remorse. She was in a bad mood and was missing her dad so much. In her eyes, poor Catherine was seen as an intruder. She did not like them all sharing the same gifts.

Maria went in to get them ready for school but heard Cecilia telling her sister not to treat other people badly. They were lucky because their parents chose the city and that they worked very hard to make them happy. Catherine's parents worked on the farm and that was not her fault. Maria asked what was the matter? They both responded simultaneously, "Nothing mum."

"Where is Catherine?" "She is in the toilet in the guesthouse. She has a stomachache." She hurried Alice to take her shower, so she could wash her sister and Catherine.

When it was Catherine's turn, Maria had to go get her from the guesthouse. She sat in a corner in the bedroom crying bitterly, her eyes were red and swollen. Maria was shocked. Why didn't you come to tell me that you're not well? Cecilia said, "You have stomach pain". She nodded. She picked her up and took her to the main house and gave her one tablet of Panadol with a cup of lukewarm water to drink and wiped her tears away. She was afraid of snitching on Alice. They got ready for school, but poor Catherine was afraid of getting into Maria's car. Alice's words that morning had had a terrible impact on her. She sat in the far corner trying not to get in her way. They all carried the new bags Joe bought for them from China.

At school, she walked slowly to her classroom, greeted her teacher and sat quietly at her desk. She was not her usual bubbly Catherine. Everyone noticed the change in her. She told her teacher that she was not feeling very well, but she wanted to be in school. A school nurse was informed immediately. She took her to the sick room and checked her over. A bit of fever, nothing to worry about. She gave her a sugar salt solution to help with the stomach issue. After an hour, she was feeling much better and was allowed to continue her lessons. During lunch break she kept to herself in the playground. Cecilia went to see her and spent some time with her. They talked about school lessons. She was grateful. Alice was busy showing off her new nails and telling her friends about the Spa break.

Joe's driver had returned to Bo, so Maria asked him to pick up the children after school. While waiting at the school gate, a teacher walked up to the car with Catherine's medical report. She handed it to the driver to give to her guardian. "Get well soon!" she said to Catherine who had got in the car. And then she went back to the office. Alice and Cecilia got in the car, and they went home.

Maria was out grocery shopping when they got home. They freshened up, changed into their house attire, and did their assignments. Cecilia helped Catherine with the bits she struggled to do. When they finished their schoolwork, Alice and Cecilia watched their favourite cartoons. Catherine went for a nap in the guesthouse. When their mum returned, the driver handed her the school medical report. The document was just for information only.

She went in, and her daughters greeted her. She went to their bedroom to look for Catherine, but she was not there. She knew where to find her. She asked Alice to go and get her from the guesthouse. When she got there, Catherine was lying down in the dark. "Mum asked me to come get you, little peasant," and she walked away. She was definitely on the war path. Catherine was scared of her. She got up and went to the main house. "Good afternoon, aunt Maria." "What is the matter? Why did you go back to the guesthouse? How's the stomach pain?" Catherine responded, "I feel much better now, thanks". Maria called her daughters to join them for dinner. After eating, they took the dirty dishes to the kitchen. Maria asked them to sit down for a short chat.

She asked all three of them to tell her what exactly happened in the morning. She heard everything. If they didn't tell her the truth, they'd be grounded and, also, no television for a month. "I will start with Alice. Tell me what happened this morning." She said Catherine entered the bathroom to use the loo when I was brushing my teeth. "She does not have manners. Therefore, I told her not to do that again."

Maria turned to Cecilia and asked her, "Was that what happened? Well, Mum. I was in the bedroom when Catherine ran in. She told us that she had a stomach ache. I heard Alice telling her to go back to where she came from. And something about our parents' wealth. I did tell her not to treat people badly because of their circumstances."

She then asked Catherine what happened. 'Aunt Maria, I would like to go back to the village at the end of this term. I thought everyone was kind here, but I was wrong. Aunt Maria, your family have been very kind to me, but if it makes your daughter unhappy, I could work for you as a housemaid. I would use the money to pay my school fees. If you let me stay in the guesthouse for the time being, I would be grateful. Thank you for all your support given to my family."

Maria was lost for words. She felt that she had just failed as a mother. Catherine's plea hit her so hard. She told Cecilia to take her cousin to the room. She wanted to talk to Alice in private. She was annoyed with her daughter, but she tried to control her temper. She talked to her daughter about kindness. She told her that Catherine's mum was very good to her when they were growing up. Life was difficult when she first met Joe. There were days they went without proper meals. Martha was always there for them. During harvest, she sent foodstuffs to them. When she was pregnant, their dad worked three jobs. Now, life has changed for them as a result of kindness from friends and relatives, hard work and dedication. "Be kind to everyone you come across. You never know when the tables might reverse." Maria asked her to apologize to Catherine. Alice did feel a little remorse after what her mum had told her. She went to the room and hugged her cousin and promised not to be rude to her anymore. They all went to sleep.

Chapter 16 - Bullying Not Allowed

The next morning, when they woke up, Alice had taken a shower and brushed her teeth as always. Despite what Maria had told her the previous night, she was still angry, especially having to apologize to Catherine. At school, she told her friends that she wanted Catherine gone. "Why?", they asked. "The little madam has forgotten her place in society. She is in the way and behaves like our equal. She gets the same gifts as us, sleeps in our room and uses our bathroom." "Someone is jealous of her little cousin," a boy who heard the conversation commented. That made Alice very annoyed. 'Alright girls, let us continue the conversation later."

During playtime, one of the girls saw Catherine playing on the swing on her own. She went close to her and looked around to see if no one else was there. She pushed her and when she fell on the ground, she kicked her on her leg and ran away. Catherine cried out. The gardener was cutting the grass and heard someone calling for help. He rushed to the play area and saw blood on the little girl's leg. She was laid down on the dusty ground. The gardener got help from the nursing station. The nurse cleaned up and dressed the wound. Catherine was given a walking aid to help with her mobility.

The headteacher was informed of the incident. Catherine was bullied by a student. She was older than her and she did not know her. Bullying was not tolerated in that school. They checked the security camera and saw the culprit running away from the scene. It captured the whole event. One of the teachers recognized her immediately. That's Janet! It was unprovoked. 'Why did she do that to Catherine?', the teacher exclaimed. They decided to watch the earlier tape that morning. They saw Alice and some students, including Janet, gathered around the corridor, but the audio was not good, so they did not hear what they were saying.

The school secretary was instructed to invite Catherine's guardian and Janet's parents as a matter of urgency. When Maria and Janet's mum arrived, they reported to the headteacher's office. The secretary acknowledged them. She told them that the headteacher was waiting for them. Catherine, Alice and Janet were also in the room. "Come in ladies! Sorry for the short notice. We have a serious matter at hand. This sort of behaviour is not acceptable in this school. Today Catherine was pushed and kicked by another student. It was an unprovoked attack. Janet, please can you tell us why you behaved in such an atrocious manner?"

Janet seemed taken aback. "Me? Madam, I don't know anything about it." Janet cried out. The students were unaware the camera coverage extended to the play area. "Really?" Janet was not just a bully, but also a liar. Janet's mum was upset about the line of questioning. She interrupted, "Do you have any proof that my daughter was involved?" The headteacher asked Alice, "what did you say to your classmates in the morning in the corridor by the school lockers?" "Just about school activities", she replied. "Well, no one is telling the truth here." "Alright, Catherine, how did you get

that cut on your leg and the bruises on your back?"
"I was the only one on the swing in the play area when Janet saw me. I thought she was going to join me, but she pushed me, and I fell on the floor. Then, she kicked me hard on my leg and ran away. I was scared of her. The gardener heard my cry and came to my rescue."

"That is a false accusation. It was not me madam. You've got the wrong person." Janet shook with feigned innocence wrongly accused of a crime she did not commit. The headteacher said, "Janet, I'm going to suspend you for two weeks if you don't tell the truth".

She called the secretary to bring in a copy of the security tape. They watched it together on the computer. When the truth was revealed, Janet's mum immediately went on her knees asking for forgiveness. She told her daughter to do the same. "When did you start inflicting pain on people? You were brought up to respect your elders and love your peers. Why did you do it? Now you are going to suffer the consequences of your actions."

The headteacher told them to get up and sit down. She continued, "Now tell us why you assaulted this young girl?". She looked at Alice and then Catherine. Alice's eyes were full of tears. Janet's heart was pounding heavily because she was about to implicate her best friend. She stammered out her words. "Alice is not too happy with her cousin Catherine staying with them. She wanted her gone. I'm so sorry Catherine." Now, she was remorseful. Alice was asked to apologize. The two girls were sent to the detention room where they spent the rest of the day reading. As an added punishment, they would clean the playground after school for a week.

The headteacher gave the parents a warning letter and any medical expenses would be met by Janet's parents. Maria was speechless. She did not believe Alice would be that malicious after talking to her the previous night. She must be spending time with unsuitable friends. She asked Catherine if she was alright? She took her to the family doctor for further examination and treatment. Janet's mum left the school feeling demoralized. Her daughter had brought shame on them. Janet's dad was a prominent figure in the community. He owned several businesses around the country. She was the only child and a very spoiled one.

Maria took Catherine to the doctor. Her leg was scanned. She had a dent in her tibia. That would take time to heal, the doctor confirmed. She did not need surgery because she was still growing. Healing could be between five and eight weeks. The doctor wrapped the leg with a cast and used two boards on each side of the leg to hold the bones in place. At home, Maria made Catherine a cup of hot chocolate and gave her some cookies. She watched educational videos on YouTube.

Chapter 17 - The President's Medical Surgery

Thousands of miles from the school yard, the President was about to be wheeled into the operating theatre. A team of five highly skilled surgeons led by Dr Jan Goldstein would perform the surgery. Dr Goldstein and his team were the best in the world. They had worked for renowned institutions and hospitals around the world. Joe was in the hospital supporting the President. He assured him that the surgery would be fine. An anaesthetist and a nurse came into the room. They needed some privacy with the patient. He insisted that Joe stay in the room. The nurse gave him the consent form. He asked Joe to fill out the form, which he did, and handed it to the President to sign. The nurse took the form, and the anaesthetist administered the anaesthetic through an intravenous fluid drip. The final preparation was done; pressure, heart rate and his vitals all checked. He had neither eaten nor drunk since twelve midnight.

He was a brave man in his early fifties. He quietly dozed off under the effect of the anaesthetic and the theatre nurses and a porter pushed the trolley to theatre one. Joe was asked to change into scrubs before observing from a glass separation in the operating room. The president had requested for him to be present during the surgery. Everyone washed their hands thoroughly and sanitized them.

The hygiene protocol was of the highest order. Joe observed through a glass partition. It felt like he was inside the room with the surgeons. There were multiple video screens all around the room. They had three student doctors also observing. The President had agreed to their presence.

It was time for Dr Goldstein to commence the procedure. He asked one of his senior surgeons to perform the first incision. The surgery was a bit complex. The cancer had spread to another organ. The lead surgeon carefully removed all the tumours from his lungs and liver. At one point, his heart rate dropped so badly but it was stabilized immediately. They thought they were losing him. Dr Goldstein instructed his team to close up, took off his scrubs and washed his hands thoroughly and went to his office. The team wrapped up. The President was taken to his private room. He was still sleeping. Joe thanked the team for saving the President's life. He was a bit exhausted, so he stretched his body on the sofa and dozed off.

It was time for the doctors' hospital rounds. The President had just woken up. He was offered a cup of tea. He was only allowed liquid and soft food for forty-eight hours. Joe requested custard with milk and no sugar for the patient. He requested a cup of black coffee for himself. Dr Goldstein inspected the patient's file and wrote a note in it. With his raspy but authoritative voice, he said, the procedure was complicated because the tumour had spread, but they had managed to remove everything. You need to rest for a week before flying back home. We can offer you radiotherapy while you are here. It was just precautionary. The doctors moved on.

Joe went out of the room to make a phone call to his family. His wife answered the call. "Hello honey! Hope you are all doing great? I was just calling to check on you and the children and also, to inform you that our stay here in Germany has been extended for a week." Maria was so excited to hear from her husband, especially with everything that was going on with Alice and Catherine. "We miss you! The girls are doing great. Catherine had an accident at school. Nothing to worry about. The doctor said she was going to be fine". Maria did not want Joe to concern himself with trivial stuff at home. Joe responded. "Alright darling. I've got to go now. Speak to you tomorrow."

The President was still drowsy and in so much pain. He had intravenous fluid and blood transfusion at the same time. By the morning, he felt stronger. He sat up in his bed and chatted with Joe. The pain had subsided due to the high dose of liquid pain relief. The doctors came into the room and were surprised to see the patient awake and sitting up chatting. "You're making very good progress" commented one of the junior medical consultants. His wounds were healing nicely. They ordered him some mashed potatoes with boneless fish stew and custard cream dessert. "Try to consume at a minimum two litres of water a day."

At the end of the week's stay in hospital, it was time to fly back to Freetown. Dr Goldstein was in the hospital at six in the morning prepping for a major surgery. This time it was a heart bypass and the patient's identity was not disclosed. The doctor went up to see Joe and suggested six monthly checkups. He had contacted his German counterpart, Dr Frankstein, based in Monrovia to keep in touch with the president. He would fly to Freetown every two weeks to ensure the wound was healing up properly, and he was responding well to the medicines. He wished the president very good luck with his health. He needed bed rest and less stress. Before returning to his office, he instructed the doctor in charge to take care of the patient until his departure. His medication was ready and a wheelchair to take him to his jet.

At ten in the morning, Joe and the President left the German hospital and flew back to Freetown. The jet landed in his compound where his wife and children were waiting patiently. Joe had phoned the President's wife and told her that the husband had minor surgery done during the check-up. The details were not disclosed at the time of the call. The family thanked him for his service to the President. Joe stayed two nights in Freetown before heading back to Bo in a government-assigned vehicle with a dedicated driver.

He had signed the contract to work as a senior personal adviser to the President. He was given an official bungalow in Freetown. He had already started his duties. His job required him to spend three days in Freetown and then work two days or more depending on the scale of responsibilities either in Freetown or Bo. It came with very good salary and benefits. It was a fair deal, and he was delighted.

His first task was to advise on what measures the government should take regarding the government officials and their men who attempted the recent coup. Joe would organize a cabinet meeting in two weeks to get everyone's input. By then, the President would have regained some strength. A cabinet reshuffle was imminent. The alleged culprits would be prosecuted by the judiciary.

Joe arrived in Bo in the late afternoon. He stopped by his office to sign a couple of documents his secretary had prepared. At home, Catherine's leg was healing well. Alice was not allowed playtime. When Joe went home, Maria gave him a rundown of what was going on with the girls. Joe was extremely disappointed. He had thought his children were well-behaved and accommodating. "Alice!", he exclaimed. "Come here. I would like you to tell me what has changed. She is only seven years old. Did she offend you?" "No dad," she replied. "I liked our small family. Catherine should not be living with us. She can visit for short breaks."

Joe and Maria told her to kneel facing the wall until further notice. The couple went to their bedroom to decide what to do next. Maria cried loudly, believing she was raising a monster. Later in the day, all the children were invited to a family meeting to discuss the way forward. Catherine pleaded with her aunt and uncle not to continue punishing Alice. She said that it was a silly mistake and with time she would get over these feelings. Catherine was very understanding and had learned to forgive easily.

Chapter 18 - Catherine's Return To The Village

By the morning, the news of Catherine's accident had reached the village. Mrs Boima, her teacher, inadvertently told a neighbour, Mary, who happened to be a very close friend of Martha. She was concerned about Catherine's wellbeing, so when someone was leaving for Bumpeh she sent a message to be passed on to Martha. Unfortunately, the story became much exaggerated in the telling. John was angry at the thought of his daughter being treated so badly. He cried out, "My poor Catherine," and slammed the door to their bedroom so hard one could see the straws from the roof of the hut lifting. Martha laid down in bed trembling ferociously. She had a high temperature with a terrible headache and her blood pressure was very high.

Joe instructed Brima to travel to Bo immediately. Martha wanted to go with him but couldn't get out of bed. She tried getting up but was dizzy. Nancy was by her mum's bedside wiping her face with a warm towel. Abbie was in the kitchen cooking fish pepper soup for their mother. John was only focusing on how to bring his daughter back to the village immediately. The story that was relayed made out that Catherine had suffered a fracture and wasn't able to walk. They would use traditional herbs to cure her broken bones if they had to.

He thought, Catherine would be safe in the village. They'd heard of bullies in big towns and cities doing terrible things to the less fortunate. Nancy narrated a story about a ten-year-old boy being continuously bullied in Bo town by his schoolmates because he had a different haircut. He could not take it anymore, so he had committed suicide. "That's a terrible story" John commented. Catherine's dream would be shattered by the turn of events especially if she was brought back to the village, but her happiness was very important to her family.

Brima made the long and laborious trip to Bo. When he finally got there, Maria had taken Catherine to the doctors to check on her leg. Joe was at work in his office in town. Alice and Cecilia had gone to school. The security guard let him into the guesthouse. The house help offered him some light snacks and water. After nibbling, he lay down on the large sofa. Joe's driver dropped the girls off from school. They seemed very happy together. They went in, washed, and changed into clean clothes.

Maria and Catherine also drove in from the hospital. Brima hurried out when he heard Maria's voice and greeted her, "Good afternoon, Maria". "Brima, you again! What brought you here this time?", Maria asked, a little surprised. He suddenly caught sight of Catherine's foot in a cast with a walking stick and limping next to her aunt. "So, it was true that you were bullied in school." Maria was astounded by Brima's remark. "How did you know about that?" She asked. "Well, bad news travels fast, Madam"

When they went into the main house, Maria instructed everyone to go wash their hands and get ready for the evening meal. The girls were hungry. Catherine asked after her mum, dad and siblings.

Maria asked him again, "why are you here?".
"John and Martha would like to thank you and
your family for taking care of Catherine and
appreciate all your kindness. They had heard that
Alice did not want their daughter here and got her
friend to beat her up in school. The family would
like me to take her back to the village." Tears
rolled down Maria and Cecilia's faces. "We really
don't want her to leave. It was a mistake. They are
just children. It will pass." Alice was excited upon
hearing this. She had won. Without thinking, she
shouted, "Yes, go back to where you belong, filthy
villagers". "Wow, get up and go to your room
now!", Maria shouted. She was horrified by the
insults from her daughter. Brima and Catherine's
eyes were wide open, and their hearts were
troubled. They left the dining room and went
outside.

Maria tried hard to convince Catherine to stay so
that she could fulfil her dream, but the environment
was toxic, and she did not wish to be in the same
house as Alice. The snide comments were
relentless. Her cousin had made her depressed.
She had no choice but to return to her beloved
village. For her, it was time to leave.

Maria phoned Joe's office to inform him that Brima
had come for Catherine. His secretary had
answered the call and quickly told her that he was
in a meeting. After the meeting, Joe called his
wife. "Is everything alright at home?" "Not really,
Brima was sent by John to take Catherine back to
the village. Alice was also very rude to her again.
The news has spread quickly in the village, and I
understand that John is furious." Joe asked, "how
did Catherine feel about it?". "She is scared of
Alice and has expressed an interest in returning to
the village." "Alright, they can leave in the
morning. It has gone too far." Joe was too busy to
deal with family issues at that time. When he got

home that evening, the family had already gone to bed.

In the morning, Maria informed the school that Catherine was moving back to the village indefinitely. Her luggage was packed the night before with all her belongings. She was very sad that her niece she loved so dearly was coming to the end of her time in Bo. She felt that it was somehow her fault that things had not worked out. She had a terrible headache from sobbing all night. Her eyes were swollen, and her face drawn with pain.

They were about to leave when Joe came out of the room, kissed Catherine on the cheek and gave her an envelope to give to her parents. She thanked him and Maria for their warm hospitality. She hugged Cecilia and waved at Alice. Before they left, she addressed her cousin by saying, "Today the sun shines brightly on you, but don't forget tomorrow it could be someone else". She smiled at her cousins and walked slowly to the car. Maria gave them a ride to the station and helped Catherine out of the car onto the bus. Brima carried the luggage and handed it to the bus conductor to store in the compartment.

It was mid-week. The bus ride to Bumpeh was smooth with few cars on the roads. Catherine was tired from a lack of sleep the previous night. She laid her tiny body on Brima's lap. Maria had given her some pain medicine before they left. When they arrived in Bumpeh, Martha and John were waiting for them in a hired car. Martha was feeling much better now. They drove to a nearby guesthouse and had dinner at the restaurant. Catherine handed over the envelope to her dad. That was from Joe. He took it and put it in his pocket. He didn't care for those people anymore.

The following day, they took Catherine to the local hospital for a doctor to advise them on her injuries. After consultation and some tests, she was prescribed antibiotics and painkillers and requested to come back in three weeks to remove the cast. The hospital bills were settled, and they left for the village. When the car dropped them at the junction leading to the paths to Giya, John lifted Catherine and sat her down in the luggage wheelbarrow. John and Brima took it in turns to pull the cart. Catherine was very sad that her dreams had been dashed and at the same time excited about going back to live with the people who truly loved her.

When they arrived in the village, Nancy, Abbie and Caroline were waiting for them in the house. They had prepared Catherine's favourite dish; cassava leaves and steamed brown rice. Caroline ran towards her sister. Catherine got out of the wheelbarrow to embrace her firmly. They went to the house, and she told her family about her experience in Bo. They were shocked to learn that Maria's daughter could be so unpleasant. They sat down to enjoy the food. It was like how it was supposed to be. "Good old days!" Catherine remarked.

In the evening, the neighbours gathered around the fireplace as usual. It was story time. Catherine limped with the aid of her walking stick and joined them. Everyone wanted to know about her experience. They felt so bad for her. She told them the stories of the armed robbers, her welcoming party, her first day at school and their spa weekend. She had good memories. She could read and write a little. She brought her schoolbooks to continue learning and improving her knowledge. She was determined. There would be other opportunities.

Back at Joe and Maria's house the atmosphere was gloomy. They had failed to protect Catherine. Joe kept in his room thinking about what had just happened in his household. He had just accepted a job to advise the President of the country, but he couldn't keep his own home in order. His ten-year-old daughter was defiant and very rude. He did not believe in corporal punishment. The softly, softly approach had not worked. His distraught wife was in the lounge. They decided that Alice would stay home for one week helping with the cleaning of the house and around the kitchen. She was a very spoiled girl and needed to learn to be kind.

Chapter 19 - Family Time And Weddings

Very little had changed since Catherine had left. It was dawn and the birds were chirping merrily in the nearby bushes. Martha and Nancy woke up early to get breakfast ready for the family. John had gone for his morning walk. The twins were still sleeping. Martha opened the window in their bedroom to let in fresh air. The sky was blue, and the sun was up. When John returned, he went to check on Catherine. She woke up when John pushed the door open. He greeted his children. "Hello my beautiful princesses. Hope you slept well?" "Not really" Caroline responded. "The mosquitoes kept me up till very late last night. Someone may have left the front door open to let them in." She missed the bedroom in Bo where there was air conditioning and only the occasional mosquito.

Martha went to get Catherine ready for bathing. They had to prevent the cast from getting wet. She was in pain that morning. They helped her to the washroom. Martha poured some hot water in a bucket then cooled it down with some cold water from the drum. Catherine sat on a bench. She applied soap on the towel and used it to wipe her body. She helped her brush her teeth and wiped the water off Catherine's body. She applied petroleum jelly on her and gave her a clean set of clothes. Then it was Caroline's turn. Martha took her to the washroom and helped her wash. They sat down to breakfast. Catherine's brothers and their wives were all present. They had a great family morning.

In the afternoon, the men changed into their colourful outfits. They all went to a traditional wedding ceremony in Timidi, the village situated in the east of Giya. The couple had travelled from the United States to get married in the presence of their families and friends. It was a beautiful, sunny day and the families were expecting a huge crowd.

John and the men took palm wine and two big bags of yam and groundnuts as gifts. When they arrived in Timidi, it was buzzing with people and loud music. Food was in abundance and lots of drinks. A professional photographer captured the event with beautiful shots and recordings. The couple arrived in two different luxurious cars in Timidi, on the main village road followed by their friends, the best men, groom, and bridesmaids in five Mercedes Benzes.

A lot of money had been spent on the wedding ceremony. The proud parents of the bride and groom welcomed everyone for honouring the invitation. The ceremony commenced with the chief and the elders of the village and its surrounding elders in attendance being served water and kola nuts. Two throne-like leather chairs decorated with gold ornaments were placed in the centre of the gathering. Zayne, the groom, was seated first. He was smartly dressed, fair-skinned, elegantly tall with piercing blue eyes. He was the son of Mr & Mrs Sam Bukai. The mum was mixed-race, from a British mother and her dad, a Sierra Leonean, who had married his mum when they both met at Cambridge University. Both studied politics and had worked in the cabinet office in Downing Street. They moved back to Timidi as part of their retirement plans, six months in the village and six months in London.

The event continued with the master of ceremony (MC), asking the crowd to be quiet. As part of the tradition, young girls disguised as the bride were presented to the groom as roses. He had to select his bride from the queue of fully covered ladies from head to toe with a thick veil over their faces. The groom inspected each of them carefully and rejected all of them and waited patiently for his bride. As soon as she appeared, he smiled and got up to embrace her and lift her veil. He led his bride to her seat. They both sat like royals in the midst of their guests. Joanna, the bride, was a beautiful slender lady, with medium height and a fair complexion. Her parents were from Timidi and had been childhood friends of the Bukai.

The groom's parents presented a small calabash filled with kola nuts, jewellery, a large brown envelope with dollars in them, thick packets of hundred dollar bills, addressed to various members of the bride's family. The family went away to view the contents of the calabash and noted them on a piece of paper. They handed the envelopes to the MC to give to the recipients. There were envelopes for the bride's parents, uncles, aunts, sisters, brothers, cousins, best friends to name a few. The bride's family thanked them and welcomed them to the family. With all the excitement regarding financial gifts, some recipients sang lustily, *"Marade dae here!" "Yawo mammy don answer yes oh!"*. Translated in English, "Do we have a wedding here?", "Bride's mum has accepted the marriage and given her consent". The drums sounded at the same time.

The kola nuts were split into halves and distributed among the elders. The couple shared one. A glass of water was given to the groom to give to his bride to drink as a sign of his love and vice versa. The Muslim prayer was led by the village imam and the Christian prayer by the pastor from the bridal party. It was a joyous occasion. There were masquerades and drumming all night. The after-party went on till the next day.

John and his entourage from Giya enjoyed themselves. They left the ceremony just after midnight. The journey back home was five miles on foot in the dark. They had torches and lanterns, and the sky was clear. They sang songs and made funny jokes. When they arrived in Giya the women and children were celebrating Catherine's return around the fireplace in the early hours of the morning. The women were also waiting for their husbands to return from the wedding in Timidi.
Martha cooked jollof rice and goat meat stew and had invited everyone. They drank ginger beer, and the adults had rum. She wanted to celebrate her daughter's return. The family deserved some excitement. No one had died. She hoped Catherine would recover quickly from the trauma. Sometimes she was very pensive and seemed lost. Martha was determined to make her children comfortable. Her daughter had quickly adjusted to the village setting.

When John and the men from the village arrived, they did not expect to see anyone still awake. Catherine saw her dad going in the direction of the crowd. With her soft and distinct voice, she called, "Dad, you're back!". "Hope you had a great time. I have really missed you whilst I was in Bo". John hugged Catherine and Caroline at the same time and told them he missed them. "Why are you not in bed?", he asked. Mum organized a small party for me. He turned to his beautiful and supportive wife and pulled her towards him and kissed her on her cheek. Martha was amazed how affectionate her husband was that morning. He thanked Martha for the party. It was getting very late, so the neighbours thanked Martha and went home to sleep. John helped Martha put out the fire, and they walked hand in hand into the house. The twins were in bed when the parents went into the house.

Chapter 20 – Revisit The Hospital

A couple of days later, it was time for Catherine's hospital visit in Bumpeh. Martha had asked Brima to go and arrange a taxi for the day. On the morning of the appointment, they got ready very early and left the house. Brima pushed Catherine in the wheelbarrow to where the car was parked on the other side of Giya. When the driver who had dozed off in his car heard a knock on the window, he jumped up and went out to help lift Catherine out of the cart, then sat her down in the rear seat. He placed the wheelbarrow in the trunk of the car. "We are going to the hospital, and it could take up to two hours. Please could you come to get us." Martha instructed the driver. He nodded his head and left.

Martha, Brima and Catherine walked slowly down the long hospital corridor and, as they approached the reception desk, they saw the doctor talking with an older woman. She seemed to be in pain as she was slightly bent over and squeezing her hips. The doctor called one of the nurses to get her a bed in the consultation room. Martha walked up to him and said, "Hello sir, we are here to take off my daughter's cast." "Yes, I remember her. Catherine?" "Yes doctor, you remember my name?" "Of course, your case was a bit different. Usually, our patients with bone injuries are older. This normally happens due to falling off trees, fights or road accidents. You're just a child. John told me when you came in the last time that you were bullied.' He sympathized with her. Catherine gazed at him for a few seconds and then thanked him for his kindness.

The doctor called a porter to bring them a wheelchair for Catherine. He took her to the X-ray department to get an image of the fractured bone. There was a long queue and when her name was finally called in by the specialist, the imaging lasted for five minutes. The porter took her back to the doctor's office. They were told to wait for the results in the patient waiting area. The doctor was treating another patient when a nurse came in with a large brown envelope. He opened it and saw the image of Catherine's bone. The tibia bone was healing very nicely. When he finished his consultation, he invited Catherine and her mum to his office. Two nurses had sanitized the tools they used to take off the cast. The external skin has healed up. They cleaned the area and gave her a brace-walking boot. She could easily take it off and put it on at home. She continued using the walking stick for support. The doctor confirmed that she was on the mend and would see her in six months. They thanked the doctor and his team and left. Brima, who was waiting in the family room, went with them to the car park. The driver was not there yet because they had finished an hour early. Martha took them to the hospital canteen to get sandwiches and drinks. They sat and waited for the driver.

Back in the village, Caroline was with her dad on the farm. She was driving birds from the rice plantation with a string and stones. She liked helping her parents on the farm. Nancy and Abbie went to fetch sticks from the nearby bushes. In the morning, they planted groundnuts and maize. The farm was large with fifty acres of land and had been passed down through generations. The vast majority had palm kernel trees and cacao.

At two o'clock, the taxi driver went to the hospital to meet Martha, Brima and Catherine. They had left the canteen early to wait for him. When the driver arrived, they quickly sat in their respective seats. Martha immediately fell asleep, exhausted from the day's events. The traffic was terrible, so the journey took twice as long. A large kerosene tanker broke down on one side of the main road, causing traffic and diversions. Catherine slept throughout the ride. The driver was also very tired. He had been up since four am. They almost forgot the wheelbarrow in the car.

When they arrived home, John and Caroline had returned home from the farm. They were drinking lemongrass tea Nancy had prepared for them. Some of the elders were playing draughts in the courthouse. The palm wine tapers had just arrived with four big gallons of palm wine. It was a good day for the tapers as they made more cash from the sales. The men had a bet on the game. The winner received a bag of rice. Every player concentrated so hard on being the winner. Eventually, one of the veterans of the game won. The men drank till late in the night.

Catherine showed her dad the new boot. He inspected and said, "I'm so pleased to see your mobility has improved drastically". She giggled and thanked her dad. Catherine continued, "I can walk without a stick!" The doctor said the walking stick was to help with her balance and to prevent her from falling over. Martha told John what the doctor said about the next appointment in six months. Caroline and Catherine played a game of Ludo, a game played by two to four players. It was the rolling of a die and using the score to move up the ladder. The game had the same concept as "Snakes and Ladders". Martha had just finishing laying the table for dinner. She asked the twins to put away the game, and they went to the kitchen to wash their hands before the meal.

Nancy had prepared boiled cassava and chicken stew with mixed vegetables at the farmhouse during the day. She had wrapped them up with two heavy blankets to keep them warm. They did not have microwaves, so that was the method used widely in the village. Catherine liked the food so much that she kept asking for more. She complimented her elder sister for such a delicious meal.

While they were having a fun time, someone knocked at the door. Martha went to the door. When she opened it, there was a lady with a box addressed to Catherine. Her name was Naomi, the niece of the headteacher at the school in Bo Catherine attended. She had been sent by her to deliver the box. Martha took the box from her and invited her to join them at dinner. There was still plenty of food left. Catherine stood up to greet her but as she moved her injured foot, she mistakenly hit her knee on the metal chair next to her. "Ouch," she exclaimed. Caroline tried to help her, but she thanked her and said no need that it was just a minor accident. She rubbed her knees and then stood up. She hugged her guest round her waist and asked, "Did you come all this way to see me?". "Yes, I heard that you were a special student", Naomi responded. The gift box had arrived by courier to Bumpeh, and she was asked to drop it off in Giya.

Catherine opened the box and was very pleased at what she saw. There were textbooks, exercise books, pencils, pens, chocolate, powdered milk, biscuits, cookies, pants, pyjamas, and a few other items. She picked up a sealed envelope and handed it to Naomi to open it. It was a card with messages from her teacher and all the children in her former class. Also, the school raised two thousand leones to help with her medical bills. It was like a blessing in disguise. She spent less than a month in school and was liked by so many people. Naomi thanked Martha and her family for the food and shook hands with Catherine and Caroline. John asked her if she would like the boys to walk her to the main road? "No, I got here on my bicycle." I chained it to the pole outside your house, Naomi responded. It's quicker than walking. I really appreciate it. She put on her helmet, switched on her torch and climbed on the bicycle. She waved goodbye and sped off into the narrow path.

Catherine was so excited about her gifts and the kind get well messages on the card. She gave the money to her dad to keep, then asked her mum to store the food items in their room. They sat around chatting for a couple of hours before going to bed.

Chapter 21 - Is The Bad Weather Impacting Christmas?

The weather was so unpredictable at that time of the year. Torrential rains were common in Sierra Leone. The thundery and heavy downpours lasted for several months. The riverbeds and streams broke their banks and caused damage to property and endangered lives. Travel and people's livelihoods were disrupted. The surrounding villages were flooded, and the roads were impassable in places. Every activity was at a standstill. The men in Giya, Catherine's village, got together to do something about the flooding. They needed to save their homes and livelihoods. Water had destroyed many of the mud houses and had flooded homes. Sandbags were thrown all around the houses to prevent the water from getting in and worsening the situation. The inhabitants brought out tools and dug gutters and pathways to channel the water away and into the bushes. It still rained heavily. The news of the floods and its destruction was on everybody's lips.

After the rain had subsided, the clearing, cleaning and rebuilding began. Christmas was fast approaching. John and his family were lucky their home was not badly affected. Every time water slipped in, they quickly dried it up. There were piles of wet cloths and they smelt of damp. Most people did not leave their homes for weeks. For many, it was a sign that the gods were angry with them.

After the drenching rains, the sun shone brightly for seven days. The water had completely receded from the communal areas. On the first day of sunlight, everyone came outside rejoicing. Catherine's injuries had completely healed up and she no longer needed walking aids. She was still careful. On that day, the village elders went to the courthouse to deliberate on how best they could be prepared for future storms. A committee was formed with a representative elected from each household to look after their interests. If the household had no able-bodied person, someone else from another family was selected to represent them.

News had come from the nearby villages that dead bodies were seen floating in the rivers and streams. As time went by, the names of the dead were revealed. They were mostly older people and a pregnant woman from the same village. They were swept off by the current of the river. Unfortunately, they were washing clothes and bathing on the first day of the storm. The waves were so strong, they were caught up in the flow and swept down stream. Some people ran to their rescue, but it was too late. A boy drowned trying to save his grandmother. The pregnant woman had two young children, playing on the riverbank who were rescued by a man who was on his way home from farming. Upon hearing such terrifying news, the village committee members went to sympathize with the families of the deceased. They took with them some financial contributions. The bodies were retrieved from the river and a funeral ceremony was taking place when the group arrived from Giya. The prayers and speech were brief because the bodies had decomposed due to the length of time they had been in water. The funeral service was brief and took less than an hour. They were buried in the village cemetery. When the Giya flood committee members went back home, they reported back to the elders the day's event.

The next day, the team went to inspect the farms to ascertain the damage from the rain. They visited the different farms one after the other. Catherine's parents' farm was the first visited. It was the land close to the village. The group inspected the farmhouse. It was a bit disorganized with broken pots and dishes all over the floor. Outside, some plants had fallen over due to the heavy wind. The team organized the farmhouse and cleaned the farm. It took about twenty minutes, and the group moved on to the next farmer's land. At the end of the day, they completed ten farmlands.

The next day, the rest of the farmland was cleared out and the badly destroyed farmhouses were rebuilt quickly. By the third day, the farmers returned to work. The elders called a meeting to discuss Christmas. The courthouse was full of people talking about the fierce storms. The chairperson instructed everyone to sit down. He started, "Ladies and gentlemen, if I said the last three months were terrible it would be an understatement. We experienced the worst rainfall for many years. Lives were lost as a result." He continued, "Today we need to select a new committee to plan Christmas". Any objections? They all nodded in agreement. The outgoing committee leaders were thanked for organizing a wonderful party last year. The selections were made, and Martha was retained as the chair of the food committee. Catherine's elder brother, Alieu would be responsible for drinks and music. They would invite the families of the bereaved and the people of that village. Contributions towards the celebrations were made by people offering goats, fouls, vegetables, rum, and cash donations.

On Christmas Eve, crowds gathered in the village of Giya. A few bachelors' eve's celebrations were taking place in the surrounding villages. Christmas was a special time for weddings and the initiation ceremony of young girls to womanhood. That year, twelve young girls ranging from the ages of nine to fifteen participated. The younger men and most times the older ones chose their wives on Christmas day. Some of these men were already married with children. It was an old tradition and an entitlement for the richer men to have many wives. The women prepared yam and pepper soup and roasted cassava, maize and peanuts. The celebration usually commences three months before the wedding day. They had had bad weather, so everything was a bit rushed. The village was decorated with bounties and balloons. A large tarpaulin was installed in case it rained.

On Christmas morning, the young men slaughtered and skinned the goats, sheep and chicken. The women used the meat in preparing the meal. Several meat dishes were made. Palm wine, rum and ginger beer drinks were stored in bottles and gallons ready for consumption. The tables and chairs were cleaned and arranged nicely. The plates, cups, napkins, and cutlery were displayed on a separate table. Everything was ready before noon. It was going to be a combined celebratory party. Everyone went home to get ready for the event. Catherine and Caroline were dressed up in matching outfits. Martha and Abbie wore similar orange lace gowns embroidered with gold around the neck and chest and the men's attire was like a long Muslim garb.

The final preparation of the initiation ceremony took place. Nancy, the head of the ceremony, had prepared the girls. The parents bought nice clothes, shoes, jewellery for the occasion. Hair stylists and makeup artists were hired from Bo to help get the girls ready for their big day. The girls were ready to go out into the world. Three of the girls were getting married on that day. The chief of Bumpeh, the grooms and the elders from the nearby villages were present at the ceremony. It was a joyous event. They started with a Muslim prayer and then a Christian one.

The drumming started, and a female masquerade normally called "bondo devil" part of the ritual. A mask was worn by a senior member of the all-female Sande society during rite-or-passage ceremonies that signify the transition of girls to adulthood. The mask carved beautifully as an expression of local ideas of female beauty, health, and serenity, led the way, and the girls followed in a queue showing off their beauty and elegance on the carpet laid down for the occasion. As they catwalked in front of the large cheering crowds, they knelt to greet the chief and the elders and then continued the walk and finally sat down together in a designated area. The female members of families and friends took to the stage dancing lustily with Nancy and her team to the sounds of the drums. They were excited about their children going through the ceremony and becoming women. The dancing lasted for just over two hours.

Then there was the selection of the wives. The chief asked the three men to stand up to introduce themselves. The first man, a thirty-five-year-old farmer, stood up immediately and spoke about his background and his wealth. He was there to choose his first wife. He went up and selected a twelve-year-old girl. She blushed and seemed very happy. There was applause. She was an orphan brought up by her grandparents. The young man took his bride to sit next to him. The other two men were old, probably in their sixties. They owned large farms with at least six wives each. They chose their respective wives, fourteen and fifteen years old.

One of the girls refused because she was being forced into marriage to a short, fat and pot-bellied man who already had nine wives. When the man walked over to her, she shouted, "No, I don't want to be married to you sir, I'm just a child!". She cried bitterly. Her dad was one of the elders. He felt humiliated. Her stepmother went up to talk to her, but she vehemently refused. The dad owed the man a huge sum of money and this debt would be cancelled in exchange for his daughter's hand in marriage. The man felt used and asked for his money. Eyes rolled and women gossiped.

Then the situation escalated into a fight. The chief stood up and asked for silence. He instructed the two men to go to his house to settle their dispute after the holidays. They bowed to the chief and sat down. The double wedding ceremony was conducted with each family member presenting a calabash wrapped in white cloth and carried by a ten-year-old girl on the head, implying purity. The calabash had the usual items: kola nuts, jewellery and financial gifts for the bride, her parents, relatives and best friends. The wedding ceremonies were conducted with rings being exchanged, and then sealed with a kiss. The drums echoed through the village and around the area.

The chief and elders were served food and drinks by the newly wedded couples before everyone else.

110

Catherine sat quietly thinking how Christmas would have been in Bo. It was meant to be her first Christmas celebration away from Giya. Martha noticed that her daughter was withdrawn and not her usual bubbly self. She asked, "Are you alright princess?" "Yes, mum. I was just thinking about the city". She would have loved to experience it, to see the difference. "Never mind," she sighed and joined her sister, Caroline, and their village friends to grace the occasion.

The chief and his entourage left immediately after the meal. He was carried by four men in a hammock. His car and motorcade were waiting to drive him to Bumpeh. The Christmas celebration continued till the following day. It was a colourful event. People travelled far and wide to be a part of it.

Chapter 22 - New Year Celebrations

After the celebrations, the people of Giya tidied up their homes and the communal areas. They had an extra week's break before returning to work. The men and women used the time to visit extended relatives in the nearby villages. Some of these people had never sat in a car. They walked long distances along paths and bushes to other villages. Martha and her family at the chief of Bumpeh's request were invited to Bumpeh for the popular new year's party. The chief's family usually organised the event to review past development and infrastructure projects and announce plans for the coming year. Also, they used it as an opportunity to invite dignitaries, relatives, and special guests. Sometimes the President of the country makes a guest appearance. Martha grew up in that household, so she and her family were special guests and highly respected by the people.

When John, Martha and the twins arrived, the compound was already full of people. Everyone beautifully dressed up. The chief had a dozen wives with countless children. The palace where they lived was pretty with magnificent gold ornament decorations. It was located in the centre of the town. They had six security guards and five bodyguards. The three chefs and two house helps decorated the compound with colourful bounties and chairs. The VIP table was nicely decorated with African styled tablecloths with an imprint of the face of the chief. The green, white and blue, Sierra Leone flags were displayed in all the four corners of the table. The framed photograph of the President if the country was also on display. The chefs took two days to prepare all the dishes for the party.

When it was time to start the event, the town crier sounded the drum three times and the whole place went quiet. Prayers were led by head Imam of Bumpeh and then the chief Priest from the Catholic Church in Bo. The chief of Bumpeh gave the New Year's Day speech, he welcomed everyone. He continued, "On behalf of my family, and I, it has been an utmost pleasure to serve you, the people of this great town and surrounding villages. We have grown from strength to strength and me, Chief Bono, a very proud man would like to continue to serve my people. The past twelve months all the goals set were achieved thanks to each and everyone of you. We worked relentlessly to refurbish the secondary school. Look at the tarmacked roads from Timidi to Bo, our major project was ninety five percent completed. It is easy to transport food items to Bo and other places increasing revenues for the farmers. Two new shops have opened selling various items such as clothes and food items. We accomplished it". The crowd applauded.

He continued, "We will seek additional funds from central government and fundraising activities to maintain electricity supply, construct more water taps, build a guesthouse or a hotel to attract tourism. The boarding school that hosted privileged children would be redecorated and an annex built to accommodate more students. We have started attracting children from the capital and from overseas, United Kingdom and USA. Parents are sending their children here to school and to learn the culture. The town is growing," he reiterated. There were plans to extend the road works to Giya, Nyago and Yoni. There was a standing ovation with everyone clapping. The towns and villages were improving.

A lady raised her hand up indicating that she would like to say something. When given permission, she stood up and greeted everyone and thanked the chief and his committee for all the amazing work. She faced the chief and elders and said, "Honourable chief Bono Jr., our great elders, women are dying from childbirth. Is there any possibility you could prioritize the construction of a maternity centre with trained medical practitioners employed with the right equipment and tools?". She gave an updated with names of five women dying in a couple of days from complications during labour. It was time for a pharmacy with western medicines to avoid counterfeit drugs and to compliment traditional herbs. They normally had to travel to big towns to buy medicine. The hospital dispensary in Bumpeh did not have medicines for the different illnesses. Another round of applause by the audience. Also, things were changing. In the past, women were not allowed to speak at such occasions. This was new because of the empowerment programme being

113

organized in the villages and towns in the country. The chief responded that he would table it for discussion at the next committee meeting. He thanked her for bringing it up.

After all the speeches, the party was declared opened. The group socialised, ate, drank and danced to the live African drums and songs. As the women gathered to talk about their respective families and lives, Martha saw her cousin, Lucian. She and her family lived in a town called Mabang. Catherine was so excited because they had not seen each other since a family gathering in Yoni. The two ladies embraced tightly. Lucian hugged the twins and asked for John. He was drinking palm wine with the chief and the other men. The wives and daughters of the chief brought out bags of souvenir gifts comprising toiletries and distributed them to women and young girls. It was a delightful day.

The children went off to play with their peers in the big hall. It was laid out with mats so they could sit or lay down. The hard a great day. The event went through the night. Some of the guests had to travel back home and the journeys were either by foot or cars. Martha's cousin Lucian and husband were travelling back so they had already arranged for a taxi to pick them up to take them to the nearest train station. Before Lucian left, she invited Martha, Catherine and Caroline to visit them so they would have a proper catch up. She would take them to Rotifunk, which was a bigger town for sightseeing.

Martha, John and the children spent a few more days at the chief's residence. Martha got on very well with his wives and children. She was a friend of his first wife, Massah when they were younger. The self-contained suite was reserved for Martha's family. Massah told Martha that her cousin chief was not in good health. They had been in and out of hospital. He had kept that quiet from the public. His eldest son was being prepared to take over if he was unable to continue his role. Martha knew about his ill health but thought he had more time. The Chief was in his early 90s and had lived a very good and sheltered life. He was born into royalty, so he did not work on the farm. Four of his children were studying in the United States and Canada. The two women wiped their tears and said goodnight. She went to put the twins to bed and waited for John before going to sleep. The following day the family and relatives met at breakfast. Catherine and Caroline were introduced to their cousins. They had a fantastic time at the palace.

When they went back to the village, John started preparing for the farm. Allieu and Nancy had already started cutting the grass. Allieu was studying the Koran to become an Imam. He called the morning and evening prayers in Giya. She liked outdoor activities. Catherine spent time reading her books. Martha lamented for her cousin, the chief. They were very close. The soil was dug up and prepared for sowing seeds. After cultivating the land, the farmers planted rice and cassava stems. The work started with the rice farm and then the cassava stems were planted into the soil in long rows of ten. John and his children worked hard on the farm. They sprayed water on the soil and then set traps to scare away birds.

After several months the crops started flowering showing good signs of growth. The next few months was devoted to the vegetable farm. They grew various crops such as aubergines, peppers, onions, potatoes, cabbages and many more. The weather was perfect for growing crops. Martha prepared the meal from the previous year's harvest. The boys had caught rabbits and skinned it. She used it to cook the soup. Catherine and Caroline went with Brima to the stream to wash clothes. They joined the other children who were playing along the waterfront. Caroline saw a tiny creature in the shallow water on the other side of the stream. She shouted, " Alligator, Alligator. This place is no longer safe". They all ran out of the water and stood on dry ground. They watched it crawl away in the opposite direction. The older people continued washing the clothes but kept a vigilant eye on their surroundings. The children played away from the stream. When Brima finished, they packed up and he dropped off the twins at the farmhouse. He hung the wet clothes on the fence and ropes at the house.

In the evening, the family spent some time together. Martha told them about the trip to Bumpeh and that they may travel to Mabang at the invitation of her cousin, Lucian. The children spoke about the alligator at the stream. John would inform the village elders so they could put a sign at the stream. That was the first time they had seen one. John suggested that it may have brought them down stream due to the recent floods from the heavy rains. Martha served them ginger beer and banana bread, the takeaway from the new year's party. They told stories and funny jokes until late at night before going to bed.

The next day they spent some time on the farm. There wasn't much to do so John organized a fishing day trip. They went to the riverbank with a net and caught a huge quantity of flathead minnows and bonga. At the farmhouse, the women cleaned the fish and placed them on a traditional smoking shed called 'Banda". It was a simple metal frame about a meter high and burning wood are placed underneath them. The process is called smoking and it helped preserve the fish from going bad. They can be kept for a long time as long as they are properly done. It went on for hours. When done Martha and Nancy waited for the fish to cool down and then stored away in a wooden box.

Chapter 23 - Visit To Mabang

Time passes. A few years later, Martha received a message to go see her cousin Lucian in Mabang, who had married a senior police officer, Samuel. She took the twins with her on the visit. Mabang is a small town with a railway line in the southern province. It had a famous bridge that led to many regions.   The train was mostly used to transport people and goods from one market to another. It was very slow and cumbersome, but it did its job. With good connections, the town had a thriving business community. They had wholesale traders selling white goods from China and Europe. People came from far and wide to buy.

Martha and her children took the long journey, changing taxis and buses, then got on the train to Mabang. It was a five-hour journey door to door. They were met by Lucian's husband who had driven to the station to pick them up. The train journey was an exciting experience for the girls. It was their first time on a train. The memories would last for a very long time. Samuel dropped them off at the house and went to work.

When they arrived at the house, Lucian had prepared foofoo with bitter leaf soup and fried plantains and beans akara, fried dough made from black-eyed beans for the family. Martha's favourite dishes. The bitter leaf sauce was rich, cooked with meats of varying kinds.

Martha and the children were welcomed and led to the guest room, where they were going to stay for the duration of their visit. The last time Martha saw Lucian was ten years ago at their aunt's funeral in Bo. She had been heavily pregnant with Catherine and Caroline at the time. Lucian was surprised to see how grown up the twins were. She embraced Martha and kissed the children on their cheeks. Martha and the children took a quick shower and changed into comfortable clothes. They washed their hands in a bowl of warm water and soap to eat the foofoo and bitter leaf soup with their fingers. Catherine and Caroline said at the same time, "the food is delicious, thanks aunty".

The two adults sat in the backyard, reminiscing about their childhood. Martha and Lucian were the daughters of two cousins. They laughed about their unique choice of men when they were growing up. Catherine and Caroline played in the garden with the butterflies and beetles. The neighbour's children gathered around the girls. One of them walked up to the twins and struggled with her words, "My name is Ethel, who are you? " That's my sister, Caroline, and my name is Catherine. We are visiting aunt Lucian. The girls invited them to play a card game. Catherine ran in to tell her aunt that they were hanging out with the children from next door. Lucian said, "That's alright, just be careful and not get into a fight." She said, "of course not" and re-joined the others. They played several games and then left them and went back inside when it got dark.

Lucian's husband, Samuel had just returned home from work. He worked at the Mabang Police Station as the deputy Chief. They lived a very simple and modest life. His wife opened the gate when she heard the car hooting. When he got out of the car, he hugged his wife and asked, "I hope everyone is alright?" She helped him take his briefcase, and they went into the house. Martha and her girls stood up to greet him. He smiled at them and said, "How long are you planning on staying?" Martha was bemused by the question. "Well, not sure, a week or two. Is it alright for us to stay? We can leave anytime." Martha responded. "Oh no", Samuel continued. "You can stay as long as you want. The police confederation is hosting a family weekend in two weeks for its officers and their families in Freetown. I was just asking because Lucian and I would like to invite you and your girls to come with us. It will be a fun day with lots of activities for everyone. The President and some government officials would also be there."

During the two weeks, Lucian, Martha and the children had a great time. They went to the markets, visited friends, went to the cinema and sightseeing. Catherine was fascinated by railway lines and the trains, so she asked for a visit to the railway station. She found the announcements of the arrival and departure of trains fascinating. She repeated, "The train on platform one is about to leave, please hold tight!". She giggled whenever

119

she said it. At Lucian's, they prepared the meals together and danced to African music. The housekeeper came in three times in the week to help with the cleaning of the entire house. The gardener visited once or twice in the month. Samuel only used security officers when he was at work and in his official vehicle. He wanted to be seen as the people's police officer. The crime rate in Mabang was very low.

On the morning of the weekend trip to Freetown, they woke up, got ready and ate breakfast together. The police driver arrived in a medium-sized open-back truck. They had two junior officers with guns seated in the back. The overnight bags and luggage were piled high next to the two officers and their young wives. As deputy chief Samuel came out of the house, the officers jumped out of the truck and saluted him. They opened the vehicle doors for him and his family to get in. He thanked his officers and they left.

The ride down to Freetown was a smooth one. It took about an hour. They arrived at the conference hall in Grafton. It had luxurious apartment blocks to accommodate everyone. The VIP bungalows were for senior officers and their families and other officers stayed in the apartments. Grafton was the police training school, so it could accommodate a lot of people. It had a capacity to accommodate up to two thousand people at a time. When they arrived, the bags were taken to the VIP bungalows and the officers picked up the keys for their various apartments. The President, government officials and other dignitaries had arrived and were in the presidential lounge. They were being served hot drinks. They were there just for the opening ceremony.

The celebrations started at noon. All the officers present dressed up in their uniforms and assembled for the national anthem. Then the inspection was led by the President, Inspector of Police, dignitaries and top government ministers. Joe was seen walking next to the President. Catherine pointed at him and shouted, "That's uncle Joe from Bo!". Martha placed her soft hand over her mouth to prevent her from distracting the crowds. Everyone looked at her with surprise. She covered her face with her hands and sobbed bitterly, then used the back of her hands to wipe the tears on her delicate face. The sad memory of Bo after many years suddenly returned. She was shattered. The police drums rolled while the pageantry continued for a while. At the end, the family members were ushered into a large hall for lunch. It was a buffet with a variety of African food. The senior officials' families were seated in a special room.

When Lucian, Martha, Caroline and Catherine were about to leave after the meal they bumped into Maria, Alice and Cecilia. "Hello ladies," Martha greeted them. She hugged Maria and kissed her daughters on their foreheads. Wow, you have grown up girls since we saw you several years ago. Catherine ran up to Maria and said, "I missed you!". She greeted her cousins. Lucian embraced Maria and her girls. Caroline stood behind her mum and said "hello" to aunt Maria. They were all very happy. Maria told them that they had moved to Freetown because of her husband's job. The children were in secondary schools and doing very well. Joe's official car waited outside for Maria and the children at the entrance of the hall. They said goodbye and left.

Lucian, Martha and the rest of the group went back to change into some casual clothing. It was a bright and sunny day. They drove to Grafton beach and spent the rest of the afternoon there. Catherine and Caroline built sandcastles and ran along the beach. Lucian went for a swim while

Martha sat underneath a tree with a glass of chilled ginger beer, keeping an eye on her children. The waves were very strong. Lucian came out of the water and wrapped her towel around her wet body. She joined Martha on the bench. She opened a bottle of beer, poured it into a glass and drank it. Lucian was also an occasional smoker. She quickly lit a cigarette and smoked quickly before the girls came back.

Back in the bungalow, Samuel took a nap. He was a bit tired. When the ladies got back, he was still in bed. Later that evening, they went to see a play in the theatre hall. The officers had put on a play about the tragedy of Macbeth by William Shakespeare. First written in 1606, it seemed to have contemporary significance, a tale of political ambition, power and violence. The children did not understand the spoken words but were mesmerized by the wardrobe of the actors. At the end of the play, there was a standing ovation.

Samuel went for a quick drink with his work colleagues and the rest of the family went to the bungalow to sleep. They cleaned their teeth, changed into their nighties and pyjamas, then went to bed.

The following day, they woke up and went to breakfast. They had scrambled eggs and omelettes. It was either toast or french sticks. They had freshly squeezed orange juice, coffee and tea. After breakfast, they went for a walk in the woods. They met other families on the walk. They had to get across a muddy path to get to the park. It was a challenge as they did not have the right walking boots. When they finally made the crossing, they were delighted and they all started giggling and giggled even more, realizing the silliness of the situation. They sat down on benches in the park and watched the birds fly pass.

They were having fun. Samuel had arranged for the driver to pick them up from the park. He was familiar with the area. They left for Mabang later in the day.

Chapter 24 - Is Catherine Staying In Mabang?

By the time they arrived in Mabang, it was past dusk. Caroline and Catherine slept throughout the journey. Samuel asked Martha if the girls went to school. She told them the story of Catherine and her time in Bo. Samuel was very angry when he heard Joe and Maria's daughter had bullied and treated her cousin badly to the point of causing an injury. "That's disgusting," he shouted. "She has deprived her of the future. I'm just disappointed. I'm surprised that as the senior personal adviser to the President of the country, his daughter treated another child appallingly, and he did not help." Martha told them that Maria took Catherine to the doctors a couple of times when it happened and Joe sent an envelope, but she was not sure what was in it. Amid the chaos at the time of seeing their daughter in a cast, John, Catherine's dad, lost the envelope. It fell out of his pocket. "We did not hear from them after the incident until seeing them yesterday. After lunch, we bumped into Maria and the children."

Lucian was gobsmacked when she heard what happened and regretted talking to them. If she knew, she would have confronted Maria and told Alice off. "Don't worry about that," Martha begged them. "We moved on a long time ago. It affected Catherine very much at the time, but she accepted that life was not going to be rosy all the time. Seeing them yesterday brought back terrible memories. We are a strong unit. Catherine's time will come."

Samuel and Lucian had three children. Two of them had married and now lived in the United Kingdom with their wives and children. Their beautiful daughter died suddenly from cholera when she was just three years old. She had been looked after by a nanny at the time of her death. The family had not spoken about her for many years.

Lucian was so upset she had had a mental breakdown. She started drinking and smoking because of that. The unfortunate thing was, she had taken care of her children by herself until that fateful day. She was a very good mum. She interviewed and hired a nanny to look after her daughter just for several hours each day. The nanny had a very good reference for the job. She had been taking care of children for over a decade.

Before Lucian left the house, she had observed her skills and felt reassured and comfortable to leaving little Betty with her. She was out for three hours. After the interview, she decided to rush back to her baby girl. When she approached the house, she saw an ambulance and the neighbours in front of her house. "What's going on?" She shouted.

In the bedroom, there were two medical personnel trying to resuscitate her daughter. They tried to hang an intravenous drip on her, but her veins had collapsed, and she was not breathing. Lucian exclaimed, "what did you do to my child? She was fine when I left her." As the tearful nanny was about to explain, Lucian fainted. When she woke up, the toddler was wrapped in a white blanket. She was not moving. Lucian shook the child with her trembling hands, but she was already ice-cold. She tried to pick her up but was stopped by one of the medical officers.

"She can't be dead, can she?" She asked. He took Lucian's hand and they both went to the sitting room. "Would you like me to call someone for you?" He asked. "Yes, my husband." They used the house phone to call Samuel. When he answered, the medical officer said, Deputy chief Samuel, 'we are at your home with your wife Lucian. Please can you come home now. It's important.' The phone went dead. He was home in ten minutes. When he realized what had happened, he went up to his daughter's corpse and cried bitterly. He ordered a post-mortem and the burial took place the following day. The nanny was reprimanded and imprisoned for five years for the death of the child.

Lucian, Martha and the girls went to visit a distant relative, Mammy Kizaya. As soon as she saw Catherine, she was drawn to her. Without hesitation, she asked if they could let her stay with her for a couple of days. She had already adopted a young boy, Sorio, almost similar age as Catherine.

Martha was not ready yet to part from her daughter. She needed approval from John, her husband, in the village. Catherine watched the children studying at Mammy Kizaya's house, so she told her mum that she would like to stay. When they went back to Lucian's house they discussed it with Samuel. They knew the old lady was a decent person and had brought up many children. They decided to give her a trial. Martha and Caroline went back to Giya with the news of Catherine staying in Mabang to further her education. John was furious at first when he heard the news. When he calmed down, he said to his wife, "We must respect her wishes".

Catherine's journey to accomplish her wishes had just begun again. She moved in with the old lady, who already had four children and an adopted son. Catherine was the youngest child at twelve years old. Mammy Kizaya and Pa Taiwo, her husband, had a huge shop in Mabang selling groceries and drinks. The shop was close to the railway station.

All the children participated in the daily chores. In the morning, the house and shop were cleaned and tidied. Breakfast was prepared and served. The children went to school. During their lunch breaks, they went home to assist in the kitchen, or sell drinks and biscuits at the railway station. They knew the arrival and departure times of the trains. After school, they went home to eat dinner and then assisted in the shop. Mammy Kizaya was also a well-known dressmaker. In the evening when they have completed their daily tasks, they settled down to study and do their homework.

Catherine found the routine was a bit overwhelming. Nevertheless, she was determined to succeed. Her dreams and aspirations needed to be met. She spent the weekends helping Mammy Kizaya in the shop and learned how to design clothes. Lucian also kept an eye on her. Catherine had someone else to fall back on if she was not happy. From time to time, Martha and Caroline visited her to see how she was progressing. Four years went by so quickly and Catherine was still with Pa Taiwo and Mammy Kizaya. She was missing her parents, especially her dad. She hadn't seen him since she left Giya.

Pa Taiwo got up early one Sunday morning to get ready for church with his family. While he was taking a bath, he collapsed and hit his head. The wife heard a loud bang from the direction of the bathroom. She shouted, "Are you alright Pa Taiwo?" When he did not respond, she called the children to check on him. They found him lying on his back with blood gushing out of his nose. He had had a stroke. They quickly rushed him to the nearest hospital. Sadly, he died after two days from a heart attack. They had been married for forty years. His death took a huge toll on Mammy Kizaya. She refused to eat and did not sleep well for years. The business was not doing well anymore. She finally closed the shop and concentrated on dress making. She taught all the children the trade.

Then Mammy Kizaya became ill, and her condition deteriorated rapidly. She arranged for her cousins to take care of Catherine and her other children. On the day of her funeral, one of her relatives, Mrs Goldsmith, asked Catherine to pack up her things. Catherine was going to move in with her and her family.

Mrs Goldsmith had three children, two boys and a girl. She worked as an office manager for an international organization. Her children went to the best schools in the country. They lived in a modern house on the outskirts of Freetown.

Catherine was treated as a maid. She did all the chores.

That relationship was cut short when Catherine got pregnant by an older man, when confronted about the pregnancy, he denied any involvement. After several years, he died from a heart attack. She was still a young girl finding her feet in the world. She was thrown out of the house by her relatives. She roamed the streets of Freetown, sleeping rough and went without food for days. She was ashamed to go back to her village. When the news reached her mum, they were devasted. Abbie, Catherine's eldest sister, had recently moved to Freetown and married a plainclothes military officer. She heard what had happened to her sister and went in search of her. When she finally found her, she asked her to move in with them.

Chapter 25 - New Beginning

Abbie's husband, Pa Jones gave Catherine some funds for a small business start-up to help prepare for her unborn child. It was a terrible time for her. Her education was at a standstill after Mammy Kizaya's death. She lost contact with Lucian and her husband. They moved to another province with his work. Everything seemed gloomy and she had failed her parents. The pregnancy was a difficult one.

When John heard that her daughter had been taken advantage of, he swore to find and kill the person. He blamed himself and Catherine's mum for trusting people and exposing their daughter to a cruel world. John was so disappointed and lost all hope. He packed a small bag and went in search of his daughter and the man that got her pregnant. His journey took a different turn. He stopped at his relatives in Yoni to say hallo to them but died from a heart attack as soon as he arrived. It was sudden and tragic but not totally unexpected since he had complained of pains in his chest to Martha in recent years. As a Muslim, he was buried the same day before the news reached his family in Giya. John's death was never mentioned in Martha's household after they mourned and celebrated his fortieth day ceremony. They could not come to terms with it. The children and their mum were devastated. Alieu, Martha's son, became the head of the family.

Caroline had grown up and started a business. She sold food items from the harvest to shop owners in big towns including Bo. On one of her business trips, she met a man, Mr Feika. He was a businessman who owned a few general merchant shops in the country. He sold everything from clothing, foodstuff and building materials. He was also a landlord with three beautiful houses in Bo. They went on a date a couple of times. She was very excited when he proposed. They had a small wedding in Giya then she moved in with him. Caroline heard about her sister's misfortune. She travelled to Freetown to see her sister. They embraced each other when she arrived. Both of their eyes welled up with tears. They talked about the incident that led to the pregnancy. Caroline promised to support her financially. The following year she got pregnant with her first son.

Abbie was a tall and beautiful lady. Dark in complexion and quite different from Martha's other children. She spoke with a calm and soft voice and was a homemaker. She carried herself so elegantly and had a handful of friends. She was a disciplinarian and very strict. Catherine did all the chores in the house. Every weekday at noon she took home a cooked meal for Pa Jones' lunch at his workplace in Murray Town military barracks.

The pregnancy was in its ninth month. Plans were in place for the birth. She had a bouncing baby girl. After a couple of months, the child was unwell. At the hospital, she was diagnosed with polio. She did not have a clue what it was, so she asked the doctor to explain. Catherine, it meant that your child has suffered paralysis and will not be able to walk or use her hands properly. She was devastated and hysterical. "How did it happen?", she asked but no one replied. Catherine did not attend antenatal classes nor saw a gynaecologist during the pregnancy. Her daughter's dad passed away even before she was born. She was a single mum with no proper source of income. The grocery business did not yield very much income.

Life was very challenging for Catherine. She single-handedly cared for her sick child with small donations from relatives. She did all the chores for her sister, Abbie and husband and sold foodstuffs on the market. She was a brave and determined young lady. Her breakthrough came on a particular day when she took Abbie's husband's food to the office.

When she arrived at the office building, a young man came out of an office. "Hello young lady, how may I help?" "Good afternoon, sir, I'm going to my brother-in-law's office, Pa Jones," Catherine replied. The young man continued, "You seemed to carry that basket at the same time every weekday for the past six months". He pointed in the direction of the office and went back to his office. "Thank you, sir!", she muttered and walked away. Pa Jones was already waiting in his office for his lunch. She put down the basket and unpacked its contents on a separate desk. There was the main dish, a plate, spoons, a cup, a bottle of Guinness and napkins. She arranged everything on the corner table and waited patiently for him to eat his meal. When he finished, Catherine took the dirty dishes back home and wiped the desk clean before leaving. That was a daily task. Her travel time was an hour on the public bus. Pa Jones was rejuvenated by the meal.

When she was about to leave on that day, the young man she met at the entrance knocked at Pa Jones office door with a file clutched to his chest. Although the door was wide open, he still had to knock as a sign of respect. Pa Jones looked up and beckoned him in. He said, "Mr Abdulai, what can I do for you?" "You haven't been in my office for quite some time now. You can go now, Catherine. Thank you." Abdulai interrupted, "Sir, I came to see you because of this beautiful young lady." "What's the matter? Has she offended you," Pa Jones asked? "No, it's a delicate matter. She has been carrying that basket on her head for the past six months. I like her very much. I would like to ask for her hand in marriage." Abdulai articulated. "Alright Abdulai let's discuss this matter on another day. Catherine you can go now." She was in shock. It was like Abdulai had been reciting those lines for quite some time now. She smiled and thanked the two men and went home to her baby girl. The two men discussed Abdulai's proposals at great length. He was invited to visit the house, so they could talk to Abbie and Catherine in a non-office environment. "You can go back to work Abdulai," he instructed.

On Saturday afternoon, Abdulai arrived at Catherine's home. Abbie and Pa Jones were on the veranda having tea. Abbie and Catherine baked a carrot cake, fried some plantains and rice akara. The large vino record player had some African songs from the album of Sooliman E. Rogie in the background. It kept repeating the Mende song, "Koneh Pehlawo Beh", translated "Please open the door".

Catherine was breastfeeding her daughter in her room. The child had been poorly lately. Abbie asked Catherine to bring an extra chair for Abdulai. He was offered rice and cassava leaf sauce with a glass of wine. He talked about the reason for his visit. Abbie told him that Catherine had a child who needed medical attention. Abdulai said that he would support her. He wanted to know if Catherine could read and write. He was more interested in how he could improve her status. He offered to help find a nanny for the child when she studied. He already assumed that they had accepted his marriage proposal. They thanked him and scheduled another meeting for the following Saturday. Abdulai was from Kailahun, the Eastern province of Sierra Leone. He worked as an accounting officer and storekeeper at the military barracks. His parents were deceased. He was very hardworking and family oriented. A very strict and maybe an overly jealous man.

When he left, they asked Catherine for her thoughts on his proposal. She was unsure at first but was very pleased about his interest in her furthering her education. She liked him. "He seems nice", said Catherine. During the week, Abbie and Catherine put together a list of items for the traditional wedding which would take place in two weeks. Pa Jones updated him on the decision and the dates for their wedding. He was ecstatic. He was so happy he started the preparation. He informed his relatives and some of his friends. He bought all the things for the wedding.

The wedding day was glorious. There was plenty to eat and drink. Martha and Catherine's brother Alieu travelled down to Freetown to attend the ceremony. The bride prize was paid to Alieu. He handed the bride to the groom as husband and wife. Catherine and Abdulai tied the nuts. She was married to a caring man. She moved in with him after the ceremony. They paid for a private physio and a childminder for baby Precious.

Catherine went to school and had vocational training. She had several jobs after her training and some of them in managerial positions. She was more beautiful than ever, marriage suited her, and her dreams were unfolding. After two years of marriage, she became pregnant with her second child. Abdulai didn't want her to work anymore. He had been checking on her at work. He complained about his wife flirting with men. He was jealous. He wanted her all to himself. Catherine was not going to allow her husband to isolate her. She had started experiencing the life she had longed for. In the mornings, she waited for him to leave for work, then she dressed up quickly and went to her job. At times, she took her office attire to change into them. She swapped her shift to leave a bit early before he returned home from his job. A friend saw Catherine in town and mentioned it in a conversation with her husband. He rushed home after work and took out his belt and flogged her all over her body. He slapped her face so badly blood poured from her wounds.

The abuse went on for several months even when she was heavily pregnant. Abdulai had changed jobs. He was no longer in the same office as Pa Jones. He had a lucrative job with an international importer and exporter. He was earning more, so his wife did not need to work. He could take care of them. Catherine's daughter, baby Precious, was being looked after by relatives and a childminder. Her health had improved so much. She was responding to treatment. The injections and physio were working. She gradually began to walk and use her hands. Finally, it seemed that there was light at the end of the tunnel for her daughter.

The beating continued. He was paranoid about anything suspicious. Catherine was not allowed to speak with anyone she was not related to. Catherine could no longer take it. He was beating her with his belts, sticks and anything he could lay his hands on. She left him to protect her unborn child and herself. She went back to Abbie and Pa Jones. When they saw all the injuries he inflicted on her, they sent for her brother, Alieu to come immediately. When he arrived, they called a family meeting. Abdulai was invited. When he arrived and saw his heavily pregnant wife, he started pulling her towards the door. Alieu, a tall and strong farmer, asked him to stop. He was desperate. He knew he was wrong and had destroyed his future with a beautiful and selfless lady. He shouted, "I am going to take my wife home". Without wasting any more time, Catherine's brother slapped her husband.

He wanted to fight him, but he realized that he was not strong enough to fight back. Alieu shouted, "Well, come fight me, you woman beater!" He was fiery and was ready to inflict pain on a man who had promised them that he would take care of his baby sister. Catherine was in tears. She had hoped for a better future. They asked her if she would like to return to her husband. She sighed heavily, looked at everyone in the room, sobbing heavily and said no. She thanked Abdulai for being there when she needed someone, but he had the temper of a tiger. She did not want her children to be orphans. Abdulai begged and promised to change. The family came to an agreement that Catherine would stay with her relatives until the baby was born in a week's time. If she changed her mind and decided to go back to her husband, then it would be her choice. Abdulai accepted, apologized and left.

In the evening Catherine had a terrible stomach pain with a few contractions. She laid down quietly in her tiny room and tried not to disturb anyone. After several hours and the pain was excruciating, she walked slowly to her sister's bedroom and knocked at the door. When Abbie came to the door she found Catherine on the floor. She had fainted and was covered with sweat. In shock, Abbie cried out for help. Pa Jones came out to see what was happening. He asked his wife to bring a bowl of tap water and a clean towel. They soaked the towel wet then squeezed and lay it on her forehead and used it to wipe the sweat on her body. The next-door neighbour, a retired midwife, Angela helped them move Catherine on to a bed and she placed two pillows underneath her bottom and legs to help with

blood flow. After a couple of minutes, she woke up and saw everyone watching over her. She asked, "why am I here?" Abbie replied, "You fainted". They gave her some custard cream with milk. The ex-midwife checked her and suggested they take her to hospital. It was already six in the morning.

Chapter 26 - Births And Deaths

In the morning, Abbie called a taxi to take them to the maternity hospital in the east of Freetown. Abdulai arrived in his car with two huge suitcases as soon as he was told that his wife was in labour. When he got there, Catherine was in the room. The receptionist gave him the option to go in and support his wife or wait in the family area. "I will wait here if that is alright," he replied. He stood outside, pacing the corridors and waiting for someone to tell him that it was alright, and the baby was delivered safely.

After twenty hours of labour, Catherine finally gave birth to a pretty baby girl. She was a very big baby with wide brown eyes. She asked if the child was alright, and the doctor said she was absolutely perfect. A nurse came outside to inform Abdulai that he could come in now to see his wife and baby girl. The excited dad went in not paying attention bumped into a glass door. When he saw Catherine looking exhausted and pale, he asked if she was alright. She smiled. He immediately went to her bedside and kissed her three times on the forehead. He wanted to pick up the baby, but the nurse in the room told him to wait for them to clean her up. She wrapped her nicely in a pink blanket then handed the baby to him. He couldn't take his eyes off her. "Pretty little thing", he concluded. He hugged her very close to his chest almost looked like she was being suffocated. Catherine gazed at him. He handed the baby back to Catherine, who was waiting patiently to cuddle her daughter. She called her Princess.

Abdulai asked for them to be moved to one of the expensive rooms. Two nurses and a porter came to help move mother and daughter to a private room. At that point, Abdulai went to his car and took the two suitcases out of the car. The proud dad wheeled them into the room and gave them to Catherine. Those are for you and the baby, he told her. They arrived last week from England. Abdulai had bought every single item from Lancashire. He said to Catherine, "One day my daughter will go to England to study". He predicted his daughter's future.

While they were talking, Catherine's niece Hawa brought a bowl of fish soup for her. She was instructed by Abbie, who visited the following day.

Abdulai went to see them every day. He had taken paternity leave as soon as the child was born. He was a very good cook and prepared Catherine's favourite dishes and took to the hospital. After a week, Catherine and her daughter were discharged from hospital. The bills were settled by her husband.

They drove home to his house. Catherine spent a couple of days with him and decided to go back to her sister's house, where her other daughter Precious was being looked after by relatives. Abdulai begged her to come back home but she vehemently refused. She had had enough of his beating. He was a good person for taking care of his family but was a jealous and abusive man when he was angry. Catherine valued her life. They could stay married for the child's sake but living separately. He wanted her to live comfortably so he rented a more comfortable house for Catherine and the two children. He visited regularly and was responsible for the daily running costs of the house.

They had the naming ceremony and invited all their relatives and friends. It was a gracious occasion filled with relatives far and wide. Martha and her son, Alieu, were present at the ceremony. Abdulai invited his work colleagues and relatives. His older brother, Massaquoi, presided over the ceremony. The second child was named Amira. Abdulai called her princess Amira. Catherine and Abdulai could not reconcile their differences. There were very good days and the bad ones ending with a fight and tears. After several years, they decided to go their separate ways. Abdulai went back to his hometown in Kailahun and married someone else.

Catherine was now at liberty to fulfil her dreams. She was grateful to Abdulai for his support. She could read and write and there was a bright future ahead. At the age of two, Amira went to live with her dad and stepmother, Alicia. Catherine visited her during the weekends, and she spent most weekends with her mum. After her vocational training, Catherine got an interesting job working as a supervisor at a renowned Petrol Station next to the cotton tree in Freetown. It was opposite the law court building and adjacent to banks and the famous Roxy cinema. She was liked by the customers for her exemplary customer service. She treated everyone with respect. Her boss was very fond of her daughters, especially Amira. She took them to cinema during the weekend. Saturdays are popcorns at cinema and the famous roaster chicken and chips later. The girls looked forward to visiting their mum at work and talking to her colleagues in the office.

She progressed to a managerial position but that was short lived. She trusted her colleagues and subordinates so much and they plotted against her and embezzled funds from the company's account. One of the staff members, who was supposed to be her deputy, forged her signature. Catherine was accountable for her department, so she was arrested and taken to the criminal department for something she did not do. She spent a couple of days locked up in a small cell until she appeared in court. Fortunately, she had travelled when the documents and cheques were forged and signed. She was found not guilty and was acquitted. The staff members involved were imprisoned for several months. She continued working at the same company for six months and then resigned.

Following her resignation, she was headhunted for a job at a shipping company. It was a great job working with expatriates from England. She worked hard because her goal was to get good medical help for her daughter Precious. The money she earned was used for her medical bills. During the weekends and annual leave, she travelled with her daughter in search of the best care. She was referred to a specialist hospital in the northern province. They were very practical, and she had physio sessions to strengthen her mobility. Catherine liked the job because it gave her the flexibility to spend time with her children.

When Amira turned ten, she wanted to go and live with her mum. Abdulai was adamant not to let go of his daughter and decided to raise the issue with social services. On the day of the hearing, he arrived an hour early in his black suit and white shirt with a red tie. He was always immaculately dressed. When Catherine and Amira arrived, he went to plead with them. When they rejected his request, he got very angry and threatened Catherine that he would make life difficult for her if she did not hand over her daughter. When the security officer saw how angry he was, they restrained and asked him to wait outside.

Amira cried and felt guilty that her parents had always quarrelled and fought for her. When they were called into the family dispute room, the welfare officers asked Amira to wait outside. The officer read the case raised by Abdulai and asked Catherine to respond. She told them that Abdulai was a good and responsible dad. The only issue was he carried so much anger. When he was angry, he would beat the hell out of his victim. She would like to keep Amira now that she had a very good job. Abdulai would still provide child support and visit his daughter whenever he wanted.

He stood up and shouted, "Over my dead body will I allow you to take my daughter away". The officers asked him to be quiet and wait for his turn. His eyes were red and flashed with anger. They brought in two cups of ice-cold water for them. He quickly picked up his and drank it all in one go and put down the empty cup. The officers asked Catherine to wait outside while they brought Amira back in the room. She sat opposite her dad avoiding eye contact. She was afraid of her dad and did not wish to be left alone with him. The officers asked her, "Would you like to stay with your dad or your mum?" She hesitated. Sweat and tears poured down her cheeks. She was given tissues by the officer to wipe her eyes. They gave her time to calm down. But she was not able to make a decision with her dad in the room.

The officers asked Abdulai to leave the room. When he left, they repeated the question. She responded that she loved her dad but was very afraid of him. She would like to stay with her mum. The officers sighed with relief because they had experienced Abdulai's temper and thought it was not safe to let her stay with him. They called the parents in, and they both sat down quietly. They asked Amira the same question and she responded that she would like to stay with her mum. They concluded and granted permission to Catherine. A document was presented, and she signed it.

On the way home, Abdulai drove past them in his Corolla and shouted that he was going to disown Amira. He had two children, a boy and a girl with his new wife. He concentrated his energy on them. Amira was sent to a boarding school the following year when she started secondary school. She was happy and felt liberated. The fighting stopped for a while. During school breaks, she went back home to her dad. Her stepmother had separated from the dad. He was bringing up his other children on his own. Amira was not very much of a priority anymore, so she was allowed to spend more time with her mum. Abdulai decided to move back to Kailahun to take over his family business and work on the plantation.

When the children were a bit older, Catherine went to visit her mum and remaining siblings in Giya. Amira moved back with her mum when she was fourteen years old. She did not want to stay in the boarding home now that her dad had moved back to Kailahun. Things were going so well for Catherine. She built two big houses in her village. She took her children during school holidays so that they knew where their mum came from and for them to learn the culture and way of life. Amira became a favourite of her aunts, uncles and their children. Catherine was very proud of her village. During Christmas, she hired a generator for the duration of her stay and especially for the events and ceremonies.

She went to Bumpeh with the children to introduced them to the new Chief, Bono junior. He had taken over from his dad. He was also a kind-hearted man. They spent some time discussing plans for Giya. She would like a road built to enable easy access to other villages. He told Catherine that he would discuss it with his team.

Chapter 27 – Deaths And Burials

Life was getting better for Catherine and her children. She wanted to give back to society, so during her work vacation, she travelled to different villages in the southern province and informally adopted deprived children. She took them to Freetown, looked after them and paid their school fees. Her house was packed full of nieces and nephews from the countryside. She also became very active in politics supporting a political party. She would campaign whenever elections were approaching, sometimes used by relatives to front those campaigns. Her difficult challenges seemed to be things of the past. She was meeting and spending time with people in high places and was invited to dinners and events organized for the President, directors, judges and government ministers. She had an influence on society. She was determined to succeed so that she could help many more people.

News about Martha's illness had reached Freetown. Catherine and the children went to be by her side. It was Catherine's worst nightmare. Her beloved mum was dying. Two days after they arrived, Martha was pronounced dead. She had a terrible headache and went into a coma. The traditional healer in the village came to see her but he couldn't help. They assumed she was dead although she had pulse. When Catherine, Caroline and Abbie arrived they hired a doctor from Bumpeh. Catherine had a sister, Marian who moved to Kono before the twins were born. She came with her eldest daughter, Fatima and son, Amidu. She married a Guinean gold dealer and businessman, who had families in Kono, eastern province of Sierra Leone and in Guinea. Catherine had visited her a few times, but her children met their aunt and cousins for the first time.

The prognosis was not good. Martha had suffered a stroke and possible aneurysm. In the evening, she stopped breathing. Her body was wrapped up in white sheets and carried away to a sacred house. The funeral ceremony was organized, and messages of her death was widely talked about. Catherine sent a funeral announcement to the local radio station in Bo and later, on to the funeral bulletin at the Broadcasting station in Freetown. People travelled far and wide with food items and money.

She was to be buried in a special grave dug in one of the houses Catherine built. When the corpse was moved to the sacred house, before the burial, the grandchildren were not allowed to see her corpse. Her role as the chief of the young girls transitioning to a womanhood group only senior members were allowed to see her.

It was a solemn moment for the family. Catherine fainted at the burial ceremony. They had lots of food and drinks for the family and guests. The drums sounded during the day for seven days. The Bondo Women's society was well represented. The heads from other villages came, mourned and stayed for a week. Catherine and her girls spent a week in Giya and left after the seventh day ceremony. Before they left, Catherine paid for the grave to be decorated with marble stone. The headstone with an inscription of Martha's name and date she passed away. Her photo to be engraved on the stone.

The driver went to pick them up. He left the van parked on the motor road and walked to the village. Fatima expressed an interest to visit her aunt Catherine in Freetown. When they were leaving Marian handed over her daughter to her sister and asked, "Catherine, please can you take your niece with you?" She was surprised but at the same time excited. "Yes, of course", she responded. They put their bags and cases in the wheelbarrow and the driver and Brima wheeled them to the van. The siblings and their children stood in a round circle holding hands. They sang Martha's favourite funeral songs in Mende and prayed. They hugged each other and wept. The Freetown group left. It took them six hours drive back home. When they arrived, Catherine's friends had organized a surprise wake in honour of Martha. She was lost for words. The compound was crowded with friends and neighbours. It went until five in the morning. She thanked the organizers and everyone present. She introduced Fatima as the new addition to the family.

Fatima was a very beautiful lady. She was tall and dark skin with long hair. She was well-trained by her mother. She cooked all the meals, cleaned and tidied the house. During her stay at Catherine's, there wasn't much to be done in terms of schooling. Amira taught her the alphabets and numbers. Catherine got her an apprenticeship at a tailoring shop. She did a six-month session with them. She was missing her mum, Marian, who was still in Giya. After the funeral, she decided not to go back to Kono. She was not happy in her marriage. Her husband had many wives so most times she felt abandoned. He spent his time in Guinea where he had his main businesses. Marian started working on the family farm with her son, Amidu. She was used to the village life.

Fatima went back to Giya to be with her mum and brother. They all worked on the farm and planted many crops. They took the harvests to the market to sell. That went on for three years. Marian's husband, Alpha Jalloh, went to see them in the village because he had taken a huge loan from a man and was unable to pay back the money. He agreed for his daughter's hand in marriage if he failed to pay the money back. He asked the family to move back to Kono, where the wedding would take place. Fatima had never met her future husband. The dad was intending to sell her to repay his debts. Marian and Fatima cried bitterly.

Alieu asked Alpha Jalloh to apologise to his family and was fined ten thousand leones, a cow, two bags of rice and a gallon of palm kernel oil. They were to be donated to Marian's family before taking her and the children away. He paid the money and

145

promised to bring the other items during his next visit. Alieu stood his ground that they would not leave until his requests were met in full. Alpha Jalloh left angrily the following day without his family. Marian and her children continued working in the farm.

It was school holiday in Freetown. Catherine bought a bus ticket for Amira to go and spend some time in the village with Fatima. She was very fond of her. She was put on a different bus route. Amira was venturing out on her own for the first time. She was fifteen years old. When she got to Mile Siaka, she got off the bus and crossed the road to catch the bus to Timidi. She heard the conductor shouting Bo, via Timidi. She paid for her ticket and handed her rucksack to the conductor to put in the overhead storage. The drive was about an hour. When they reached Timidi, she picked up her bag and got off the bus. The area was a bit familiar to her. She crossed the road and went to a shop to buy a bottle of cold water. While she was there, she asked for the direction to Giya. She lady behind the bar spoke in Mende. Catherine understood what she was saying but could not respond so she replied in Krio. She thanked the shopkeeper and started the five miles journey on foot.

She went to introduce herself to the head of the town as Catherine's daughter. They offered her food, but she declined and thanked them. She told them that she had eaten on the bus. The head sent for two of his boys. When they came, he introduced them to Amira. He asked them to accompany her to Giya. One of them took her bag and they left. She thanked the head and walked slowly in the middle ensuring she was protected. They went through two more villages and crossed a low tied river. It was different from the fast and aggressive city life. It was peaceful and serene. The monkeys and squirrels were jumping from one tree to another. The birds flew in the sky. They stopped to see a chameleon change its colour a couple of times. It was green initially and then red because Amira had a red dress on.

The boys spoke a bit of Krio, so they asked her how long she was staying in Giya. They would like to take dancing someday. She was astounded by the questions. She replied that her uncle, Alieu, would not allow her to hang out with boys. When they arrived in Giya, the boys took her to the house and told Alieu, the head of Timidi had asked them to escort her. He thanked them and gave them each corn on the cob.

In the evening Marian, Fatima and Amidu returned from the farm. Nancy had malaria so she was in her new home built by Catherine. Fatima was very pleased to see Amira. She told her about her supposed wedding. They would be going back to Kono. They embraced and Amira told her that it was going to be fine. Marian brought out the food and served it. She took fish pepper soup and boiled cassava for Nancy and encouraged her to eat. When they finished eating, Marian poured warm water into a bucket for Amira to wash. She took a bucket of lukewarm water to wipe down Nancy's body. Her temperature was rising so Alieu gave her two Panadol five hundred milligram each and repeated it every four hours. She was given bitter leaf drink for the malaria. After two weeks she felt better.

On a Sunday afternoon, Fatima and Amira went for a walk around the village. They walked through the bushes and climbed trees. They picked mangoes and ate them, sitting on a small log in silence. The sun was shining brightly so they decided to go to a stream. They were not aware of the current. They sat for a while on the makeshift bridge with their feet dangling in the water. It was cool and they were having fun, and their friendship was full of laughter.

Amira took off her clothes and jumped in the fast-running stream. She had never swam before and was unaware of the depth of the river. She had never seen a clean running stream like that. It was so tempting, so inviting. She wanted to bathe in it. As soon as she jumped in, the water took hold of her and dragged her this way and that. She did not know what to do. She was drowning. Fatima shouted, "Are you alright?". No response. She quickly jumped in and pulled Amira out by her leg. By the time they got out, both had drunk so much water. It was unpleasant and scary.

She laid Amira on her side and pressed gently on her stomach and chest. Some water came out of her mouth and nose. They laid down on the grass and waited for Fatima's clothes to dry out. They walked in solitude passed the grassy hills and huge forest. Amira was terrified and in shock. If her cousin had not been there to rescue her, she would have drowned. At the end of the school holiday, Catherine went to Giya to take Amira home. She also wanted to spend time with her siblings. Nancy was feeling much better. Catherine took with her one of Nancy's boys to stay with them in Freetown.

After a couple of months, Fatima's dad went back with the items requested by Alieu. They had a family meeting, and he gave his word to take care of his family. He travelled to Kono with his wife and children. Fatima married a man who already have two other wives. They moved to Guinea Conakry. Marian moved to her husband's house in Guinea.

Nancy continued the work her mum had started with the girls and ladies Institution. Parents travelled far and wide with their girls to go through the process. It went on for a few more years until her death from old age.

Chapter 28 - Wars And Uncertainties

Catherine was an ardent member of the main political party. There was an unrest in the neighbouring country, Liberia. A terrible war that spilled over to Sierra Leone brought terror to its people. The rebels from Liberia came through the border and recruited men, women, young boys and girls as they attacked towns and villages in Sierra Leone. They looted businesses and houses and maimed innocent people. Women and girls were taken away and raped. It was atrocious and, in most parts, extremely violent. When the fight reached Kailahun, a town in the eastern province sharing a border with Liberia, Abdulai, who had moved back to his hometown to run the family plantation and business, was one of the many people who lost their lives and properties. He and his family were attacked by the rebels. He died from a gunshot while escaping from the brutal attacks by the rebels. His body was never recovered.

The rest of his family went to Guinea Conakry and when the fighting calmed down in Liberia, they moved and settled there. It was a bloody war that lasted for several years until the British army intervened. Most of Catherine's relatives and friends were killed. As the fighting escalated, many towns and villages were attacked, destroyed and sometimes taken over. There was fierce fighting in Bo town. The local people formed a vigilante group to protect the towns and villages against the rebels. The rebels attacked Bumpeh and Catherine's village, Giya. Caroline and family were in Bo at the time. The buildings were destroyed and the houses she built were looted and set on fire. Her beloved village went up in flames.

Nancy's elder daughter bearing the same name as her mum was killed by the rebels. She couldn't escape because she was mentally unstable. The devastating news reached Freetown. The fight progressed and reached the capital. People left their belongings and fled for their lives. They went in small boats, walked long distances through the bush and forests, and the most privileged got on planes and ran to safety. The killing was indiscriminate, and they killed people like flies. They had guns but often used weapons such as machetes and knives. The drugged fighters did not care and felt nothing for human lives. They saw their relatives and friends as enemies. The Red Cross and the United Nations tried to make them understand the laws governing wars and civilians. The Geneva Convention was not observed by the combatants.

On the other hand, the military fought relentlessly to bring peace and stability. It was a tough one. The mining area in the eastern province, Kono was attacked by the rebels. They spent a long time there because of its resources. They looted and took over the mines. The money from the sale of diamonds and gold mined was used to fuel the war. They bought ammunition to help in the fighting. It was a senseless war masked with greed. The leaders did not care about the people and the country.

When the rebels took over Freetown, Catherine and her family house was targeted and attacked a few times. It was set on fire on two consecutive days, but it was quickly put out by the neighbours and passing military officers. Her life was threatened and that was very frightening. Gun men shot at the doors and windows. A bullet hit Catherine's grandchild, Janet, in the leg. Fortunately, it was a scratch because the bullet did not penetrate the skin. Catherine told everyone to lie flat down under the beds to prevent them from stray bullets. When it had quietened down, they knocked at a neighbour's door, a medical practitioner. He treated Janet's wounds and gave her an injection to prevent tetanus.

They were terrified by the constant humiliation and aggression. Dead bodies were seen lying across the roads and in gutters. Limbs were amputated. It was like a never-ending horror movie. Women,

men, children jumped over high fences and walls to escape the onslaught. She lost loved ones. Her twin sister, Caroline's son, Bobby was killed while he was running away with his family. A bullet hit him on his back and went through his chest. He was rushed to hospital by some soldiers, but he bled so badly and died on the way. His corpse was taken to the mortuary and later buried by his wife and family.

Although Catherine campaigned and supported her relatives during elections and political rallies, she and her children never benefitted from them directly. Catherine was selfless and wanted the best for her people and country. She thought with the right governance and people in power, Giya and the surrounding towns and villages would be developed, and decent roads built.

The country was in a chaotic situation, and the fighting was spreading like wildfire. The nights were long and frightening with loud sounds from heavy artillery fire and gun shots. They could see thick smoke from burnt edifices from miles away. The sky was grey, and the birds had all disappeared. The city smelt of burning carcasses. The electric cables that supplied power had been destroyed by the fighters. The city was pitch black at night apart from the lights from the military vehicles and those of the rebels.

It was time for Catherine to take that bold step, they had to go somewhere else. They had already left the house and were taking shelter in an unfinished building down the road. They stayed there with fifty other people in a small space. That was the only option they had to stay alive and from the constant threats. The rebel did not go to the unfinished and burnt down building. A rebel collaborator saw them in their hiding place and told the rebels. The young men in the hiding place formed a group to defend themselves if they were found. Fortunately, one of the rebel fighters recognized Catherine. She had helped him secure a job many years ago at a shipping company. He asked his colleagues not to kill them. The fighting men told them to find another hiding place because they were not safe. They may not be lucky if found by the next set of fighters. They went back to their houses and hid in the cellars underneath the buildings. Early in the mornings, they cooked rice and ate with sardines or whatever they could lay their hands on. Most of the time they fed on gari, made from processed cassava root and drank water. It was survival for them as they sometimes went for days without food. They did not wash for weeks. The taps were not running, and the main water supply had been polluted. Water was a scarce commodity, so they had to manage with whatsoever they had.

After a few months, the rebels had been pushed back from the city centre and a ceasefire had been agreed for a couple of weeks. The President went on air to make the announcement. There were curfews from ten o'clock in the evening till dawn every day. Some world leaders and the international community had intervened and requested for mediation. The West African peace keeping force, ECOMOG, sent forces to help the military protect the country and its inhabitants. Some developed countries sent planes to rescue their nationals and diplomatic staff.

Catherine organized a car to take her and her family to catch the bus to Guinea, Conakry. Some of her nieces and nephews refused to take the journey. They stayed in the house. She travelled with Precious and her grandchildren to Guinea Conakry. Their stay in Conakry was cut short due to language barrier, French and Fullah being widely spoken. The people they came across were not very welcoming. They were also stressed and worried about the war extending to their country. That made them aggressive and disliked foreigners. Normally, Guineans were very receptive.

Catherine's sister, Marian, was living on the outskirts of Conakry. Catherine decided to go anywhere far away from Sierra Leone, Guinea and Liberia because they all shared borders. They stayed a night in Conakry in a guesthouse and left the following day for Ghana in a commercial minivan. The journey took several days. It was arduous and difficult, but they were happy to be moving away from the violence in Sierra Leone.

But then as they went through the Ivory Coast border, their vehicle was attacked by bandits at night. They were young men who stole from travellers especially at night. The driver of the van was very skilled and knew how dangerous that area was. There had been several reports about security especially travelling at night. The driver tricked the gang by pretending as if he was stopping the vehicle when they beckoned him to stop and pointed knives at them. He waved at the gang just to gain their trust and slowed down the vehicle. As soon as they walked towards the passenger side, he sped up, and the passengers could hear the tyres screeching. It was like a formula one race experience in a van. When they escaped the passengers clapped and thanked the driver. He was shaken but he was happy and proud that he had saved their belongings and even their lives. When they arrived at the main bus station in Ghana, Catherine and the children went to the embassy to present themselves and to ask for information.

They took them to a refugee camp in the outskirts of Ghana, where they met other Sierra Leoneans and Liberians. They lived a modest life but were happy to be away from the noise of gunshots and burning smells of buildings and human carnage. Catherine was unhappy because of all the deaths back in Sierra Leone. She joined other Christians to pray for an end to the wars and sufferings around the world. Life in Ghana was terribly hard. The adults did meagre jobs for the Ghanaians working in the farms and helped with the harvest of peppers so they could earn some money to help with food and toiletries. The children went to schools and adapted to their new lifestyle. The adults could not find decent jobs.

They received some help from Amira, who had travelled to the United Kingdom, a couple of years before the fighting spread to the capital. A family took them in, so they left the camp and stayed in the city. They had lovely time with the family especially the children. Precious and her children went to the United States after five years in Ghana. Her younger sister, Amira's daughter, who was also, schooling in Ghana, travelled to the United States. Catherine travelled to the United Kingdom to join Amira. That was the beginning of their recovery from the traumatic experience of the war.

Chapter 29 - Trip to London

It seemed as if everything was coming together in a positive way for the family. Catherine's older daughter and her children would travel to the

United States of America through a repatriation programme. Their visas had been approved and passports stamped and sealed. A desperate person could translate it as 'Permission granted to the land of milk and honey'. For most people running away from political and economic instability, going overseas was like a prayer answered. Catherine was invited to visit her daughter, Amira in the United Kingdom. Her visa application was successful after two horrible attempts. The officers were not convinced that she would return, and the state would have to fund her stay. They were completely wrong. Amira and husband had good jobs, working for development and relief organizations. They owned their own home so there was no reason for government help. Catherine was a hardworking and independent lady, given her the opportunity, she would work and pay her way in society.

She was worried and concerned about the future of her family travelling to the United States. They had been a closed unit and had suffered everything that was thrown at them. For the first time, she has been separated from them. When Catherine arrived in London, Amira was patiently waiting at the airport for her mum. She waited patiently and checked the flight route before the plane landed. Catherine had some delays at the immigration desk. She was questioned by the officer about the war in Sierra Leone and why was she flying from Ghana. Her answer was that she was visiting her daughter, Amira. She got through and collected her luggage.

When she finally came through the arrival doors, she looked different. She had aged badly, was thin and looked sad. Her beautiful smiles had disappeared due to the trauma and suffering from the war. The years spent in a refugee camp and moving in with a family in Ghana had brought her many things and changed her perspective on life.

The culture and way of life was slightly different from what she was used to back in Sierra Leone. Amira had not seen her mum for several years. It was a difficult reunion with mixed feelings. Some good and bad things had happened over their lost years.

Catherine's fair complexion had gone dark beyond recognition due to the sunny and extremely hot weather in Ghana. She walked slowly in a colourful printed African dress in a pair of high heel shoes. Amira waited and waited. All the passengers from the Accra flight had come through. She asked an official but did not receive any information. She was getting worried. Then Amira saw her mum, she finally recognized her mum, she ran up to her and said, "Hello ma, welcome to London, hope you had a pleasant flight?" They both embraced and tears filled their eyes and ran down their cheeks. They sobbed for about five minutes and then smiled. There were tears of joy and sadness. They hugged again.

Amira took the luggage cart from her mum and pushed it to the taxi ramp. The journey to Amira and husband's flat in Brixton took almost an hour. The two ladies did not say very much throughout the drive home. Emotions were high and mostly repressed. Catherine gazed into her daughter's eyes and wanted to tell her all about the war and how she had missed her. She asked her, "Are you happy here?" because her daughter had lost so much weight. Amira replied, "Yes, but life is hard in London". "Now that you are here, you will understand". She had to work full time to pay her university fees, support relatives and did a part-time degree. Her husband had travelled overseas for work.

When they got home, Catherine had a warm bath. Before going to the airport, Amira had prepared her mum's favourite food. She liked meat stew, vegetables, and boiled rice. They ate dinner together and talked about plans for her stay. At night, she had terrible nightmares and bad dreams about the war. Sometimes she cried and shouted for the soldiers not to shoot. She was traumatized.

It went on for several years until she went for counselling and prayers at the local Catholic church.

Finally, the dreadful war in Sierra Leone came to an end but the aftermath was devastating. It was not considered a safe place because the ex-combatants were being incorporated into the community without proper rehabilitation programmes. After a couple of years, she decided to find a job in London, afraid to go back home to Freetown. She found a job as a housekeeper in a hotel that involved strenuous tasks. She was bored sitting at home watching television and wanted to earn some money to continue supporting her siblings and relatives back in Sierra Leone. She found a second job to complement her income. That was what most immigrants did. Some days she worked long hours just to support them financially. Her daughters told her that it was time to stop and enjoy her old age, but she was stubborn and kind. She felt responsible for her family and relatives, and they took advantage of her compassion. She would send money to support them, and sometimes had to borrow money from friends to get her train and bus tickets to work.

She was at work one day, when she received a phone call that her twin sister, Caroline had cancer, that had spread to her lymph nodes. It was stage three, but the doctors told her that with surgery and diet her chances of recovery was good. She was worried and wanted to save her sister's life. She could not travel back to Sierra Leone to be by her side because she was still waiting to hear from the

Home Office regarding her leave to remain. Her lawyer had advised her not to leave the country at that stage of the process. She sent money to cover the medical bills. The hospital in Freetown prescribed a very long list of drugs, some of them were not available in the country. Catherine bought them from the United Kingdom and sent them through a fast courier service. Unfortunately, she died after three months from her wounds. She was in so much pain and the wounds never healed. The surgery was not done professionally, and no one was accountable for it. The burial took place in Bo town with family members and relatives present.

When Catherine was grieving Caroline's death, she received another piece of shocking news that her elder sister, Marian, died suddenly from brain haemorrhage. She was found dead in her bedroom with blood gushing from her nose. Losing two sisters within a short space of time had a profound effect on her. When she heard the news, she fainted. The thought of burying her two sisters' months apart was unimaginable. "Are we cursed?", she exclaimed. She was devastated and suffered from terrible migraines. She was diagnosed with high blood pressure. The terrible news of her sisters' deaths triggered her blood pressure. It was extremely high. She was out on medication but was ill-advised by her friends not to take them.

Catherine found a job at Guy's Hospital, south of London Bridge as a care assistant. She had been trained in providing care, first aid and communication. She made friends easily and had lots of them. She was well known and well appreciated amongst her community. She rented a flat so she could invite and entertain her friends. She was happy and celebrated her birthday every year and went to parties. She was introduced to a man by a friend. They saw each other for one year and then decided to move in together. It was an exciting time for her. Amira and Catherine bought a flat in the Dulwich area. The flat was decorated and furnished. Catherine and partner, Leroy, were ready and all set to move in. In the morning, her passport had arrived in the post with the relevant leave to remain stamped in it. She was ecstatic. Everything seemed to be working for her and the family. Her daughter, Precious and children were settling down in the States. They quickly established themselves in the community in Philadelphia. Initially when they arrived, they were met by the Catholic Refugee Council, who helped them find their way around the city. They met old friends who were in Ghana at the same time and made new ones. They received enormous support from the church.

Years went by and everything seemed as if she was in a dream for Catherine. She had become a part-owner of a two-bedroom flat in the Dulwich area. She was going to move in with her partner and this was a short walking distance from her daughter and husband's house. She had regained her fair complexion with pretty hair and dressed very well. She was happy and had money to support her relatives back home. On the morning of her day off, she walked down to her daughter's house and spent some time chatting with her husband. She mentioned that she had a persistent headache despite taking medication. In the afternoon, she left to visit a work colleague, Maisy, who was admitted in hospital. When she left, she went to an hour evening job. She used the extra cash to supplement her income.

That same evening, as Catherine was on her way home from work, she heard a big sound in her head. She managed to get off the bus and collapsed on the cold pavement. The paramedics were at the scene within five minutes of the incident. Her blood pressure was very high, she went into a coma. She was taken to King's in Camberwell. When she was finally seen by a doctor and all the tests and a CT scan done, the family was told that she had suffered a massive stroke. It was a grade four aneurysm.

Amira wanted to know what could be done, so she asked the doctor. What's the prognosis? Five surgeons and an anaesthetist stood around her bed deliberating over her condition. They came to a decision and called Amira to inform her. The lead surgeon said your mum was not going to make it. If you needed to call anyone, this was the time. Go and say goodbye as she was not going to make it. We will organize a porter to take her body to the mortuary. Amira went into shock and was numb for a couple of minutes while she steered into the eyes of the men, who were meant to help keep her beloved mum alive. She pleaded with the doctors to do something for her mum. She told them that she was fine a couple of hours ago and had worked hard looking after people in her job at the hospital, so she deserved their help. The doctors looked at each other and walked away disappearing into their offices.

While this was happening, for some reason, the anaesthetist stood by Catherine's bedside and refused to leave. He was a tall and elegant young man who knew something could be done but not in the position to say. He heard what the doctors' decision was but as a protest, he stood there with some sadness in his face. This was how Amira interpreted the situation. He didn't say a word but looked at Catherine with pain. Amira was shocked and disappointed because they had refused to help her mum. She felt that something could be done and wondered what the anaesthetist was waiting for. Amira went out to make a few phone calls to family members informing them that her mum had passed away. She was full of tears and refused to accept it. When she went to be by her mum's side, the anaesthetist was still there.

She wanted a sixth or seventh opinion. She shouted so loudly that if the doctors refused to help her mum, she was going to commit suicide. When the hospital authorities heard her daughter crying and shouting, they rushed to Catherine's bedside. She explained that her mum was in a coma, but the doctors had decided not to help her. They tried to convince her that she was dying so the doctors had other patients that needed immediate help. Amira's wailing continued and she said that she was going to harm herself if something was not done.

A quick meeting was held with the family and the surgeons agreed to take Catherine to surgery. They did not guarantee a positive outcome. A nurse handed over a family consent form giving the go ahead, which Amira signed. She was prepped for surgery. The anaesthetist's face was now relaxed revealing hope. He waited until they went into surgery to administer the anaesthetic. Catherine was taken into surgery, which lasted for six hours. She was still in a deep coma. Amira went to the prayer room and spent some time there. She wanted to be alone. The operation was incomplete, but they halted the bleeding, but they drained blood and liquid from the brain.

In the morning, she was transferred to St George's hospital in Tooting which had a specialist unit. It took twenty minutes to get there, and Amira went in the ambulance with the paramedics and her mum. She was wrapped up in white sheets with hands and feet strapped together. A white bandage wrapped around her head and face. The only revealing part of Catherine's body was her eyes. She had a catheter, tubes and oxygen attached to her body and mouth. She was laid on the stretcher like a corpse. The paramedics were professional and caring. Amira could see her mum's caring attitude in them. She sighed and thanked them.

When they arrived, there was a long queue of ambulances with sick people waiting to go through admission. At the emergency department, Catherine was rushed through, and a room was already allocated for her. The family were invited to a separate room to discuss the next step. Two men walked in with a huge file. They were Canadian and British doctors. The Canadian was the lead surgeon and he introduced himself as Mr Donaldson and his colleague as, Dr Lewis. He continued, "We are responsible for carrying out the surgery. We would like to inform you that Catherine's case is very complicated". Even if they drained all the blood from her brain, she may be rendered useless. They were asking Amira to give up and let her die slowly. All the hope she had had disappeared, and she sweated profusely. She pleaded with them to help, and she would look after her mum, even if she was rendered useless. She knew her mum was a fighter and would not give up when she was still breathing.

Amira signed the consent form, and her mum was wheeled on the trolley to the theatre. She had an additional five-hour surgery. The wait seemed so long but it was worth it. News had spread far and wide amongst her friends and family that Catherine was dead. People were blaming her daughter for trying to keep her alive. When the surgery ended, the surgeons took off their gloves, washed their hands with soap and warm water with two nurses waiting to give them clean towels and helped them take off the theatre gowns. They had gloves on to help prevent cross contamination. When the porter and nurses pushed the trolley out of the theatre, Amira asked, "Is mum alright?" The extra layers of white sheets wrapped around her mum with more tubes coming out of her mouth, nose and chest seemed scary. She was expecting the worst. The nurses responded, "Don't worry the surgeon will tell you all about it". "We are taking her to ICU". She followed them to the unit but was not allowed in. She peeped through the tiny glass on the door, but all she could see was very ill patients with long tubes and catheters. The nurses and doctors were so busy running from one patient to the other. She watched them lay down her mum in another bed. They were gentle.

The lead surgeon invited the family to a private room to discuss the surgery and prognosis. He said that they should expect the worst if she recovered. The wait for recovery was long. When she woke up from the coma, she was like the little Catherine back in Giya. She had time travelled back to her childhood in the village of Giya. She did not recognize the present. It was a sad moment, but she was back from the dead. She was alive! She had beaten all odds. She spoke Mende to the nurses and doctors She had forgotten the English language and Krio, the vernacular, that was widely spoken in Sierra Leone. She did not know who Amira was. She recognized the face but was not sure who she was. Amira was grateful her mum was alive. Catherine remembered her daughter, Precious, who lived in the United States of America. With the support of Amira's husband and Catherine's partner, relatives and friends, she got better and stronger every day.

The next few years were the most difficult time in her life. She could not do anything for herself. She was in intensive care for a month and moved back to the original hospital and spent six months in the rehabilitation ward. The first time she stood up to go and use the bathroom she fell. She was badly paralyzed in one leg and one arm. The physios were immediately called to the scene. In rehab, she learned to walk. The hospital provided her with occupational therapy. She had to learn to speak again, read and write. Her mobility improved with physio and massages. She learned to use the stove to warm up her food. She was terrified holding sharp objects like knives. Her speech improved with constant practice and learning.

Chapter 30 – Wedding, Illnesses And Bereavements

Six months in the rehabilitation centre at the hospital helped Catherine in her recovery. She was determined to recover from her trauma. Her speech had improved slightly, she could lift the right arm with minimal support. The major paralysis was her right leg. She had a terrible foot fall and had wounds from dragging it when trying to walk. The entire leg was lifeless, so she was given a walking stick. The physios and occupational therapists did amazing jobs with her. At the centre, the nurses pushed her around in a wheelchair. Most of them were kind, they helped shower, applied lotion and assisted in putting on her clothes and panties.

One day, as Amira was going to visit her mum, she saw a clumsy nurse taking her mum in the wheelchair to the bathroom. She was dragging the weak foot on the floor banging against every object on its way. She didn't seem to care as she was just there for the money. Her foot was bruised, and she bled from her wounds. Poor Catherine was vulnerable, and the woman took advantage of that. Walking behind them, I could hear the nurse shouting at her. Telling her that she should take care of herself and next time she would not assist her. Amira was shocked and immediately stopped and confronted the woman dressed up in sky blue scrub. It was like a bad scene in a hospital movie. Such things happen in television dramas, not in reality. When she realised that they were related, she apologised. Amira was hurt and was afraid to leave her mum in the hands of indecent people like her. After taking Catherine back to her bed, she picked up her bag and disappeared. Amira was told that she was temporary staff from an agency covering a shift for an absent staff. She was never seen back in the centre for the duration of Catherine's stay.

The wounds were cleaned and treated by another nurse, who knew her before the stroke. He was gentle, kind, and promised to take care of her and would not let anyone maltreat her. The centre was so busy, they sometimes forgot to help with her meal. She still struggled using her right hand to use cutlery and gradually learnt how to use her left hand. When she was discharged from the rehab centre, she struggled to live in the flat they had bought for them. It was on the second floor with no lifts. The steps were narrow and uncomfortable to climb even for someone without paralysis. She fell down the stairs and injured herself and found her day-to-day movement very challenging.

Catherine was relocated to more suitable accommodation with her partner down the road in Peckham. The new home was on the ground floor of a gated community. They liked it and would help her recover quickly. She quickly established herself and made friends with her neighbours. Her partner was very supportive. He was a trained chef. He cooked the meals and took great care of her. He loved her so much despite her misfortune. She would never go back to work. They became close friends and fed on each other's strength. He was originally from the Caribbean and had lived in Canada for many years before moving to the United Kingdom. The medical team visited her at home on a regular basis, and they signed her in for sessions at the local gym for swimming and the treadmill. She worked out and was able to swim for a few hours per week and made some progress. She could walk without the walking stick around the house.

After one year together in the new home, they decided to get married. They contacted the priest of the local church of England to discuss their plan. A date was fixed, the rehearsal and preparation started. The wedding ceremony would take place in three months' time. They invited families and friends to the ceremony. On the day of the wedding, the bride was beautifully dressed in a white gown revealing her cleavage. Her hair was nicely done with a veil on her head. She wore a pretty flat pair of white shoes. The groom was elegantly suited in a white silky shirt, waistcoat, and grey jacket and trouser in a shining black pair of shoes. He was a handsome man. He had his gold jewellery, a nice necklace and rings. The bridesmaid was Catherine's niece, Julia. She was good looking and had won beauty contests in her day. She loved her aunt and wanted to help. They organised the wedding and, on the day, she woke up early in the morning to help dress the bride and put on the makeup. After the church service, the bridal team went off to change their attire. The party took place in the church hall packed with people. The long speeches went on for eternity, then eating, dancing and drinking ensued.

She married and lived happily together for many years until her husband was diagnosed with multiple illnesses. They travelled to a few countries. Her husband was ill and died from complications. She was by his side when he took his last breath. Life had never been the same for Catherine. Her best friend and pillar of support had gone forever.

After her husband's death, she revisited Freetown and Bumpeh. She was unable to go to Giya because of the bad roads. They had been destroyed during the war. The family houses were looted and burnt down in the village. She needed a car to travel around because of the paralysis. She was the only

one still alive. Her thirteen siblings died from various causes. Her dad disappeared from the face of the earth when he heard his teenage daughter was pregnant. Her first husband, Abdulai died because of the war. Her mum, Martha, passed away unexpectedly, and her second husband died from cancer.

Chapter 31 - The Reunion

Catherine's cousin, Cecilia from Bo was married and lived with her husband in Germany. Her parents were staying with them. When she got home from work one evening, Joe and Maria told her that they had contacted Catherine in London. Cecilia was delighted that they had found her and reconnected the family link. She asked, "How is Catherine? Was she pleasant on the phone? What did you talk about?" Maria responded, "oh Catherine, poor Catherine, she was polite and interested in knowing all about you and Alice". Cecilia was surprised, as she had feared that Catherine would be unfriendly and full of bitterness. It was not in her character. She was brought up to be kind and loving.

Cecilia asked her parents, "Would you like to go visit her in England?" Joe was happy about the prospect of travelling to London. He had heard that the Sierra Leone community was buzzing and some of his friends had moved to London. He would take the opportunity of visiting his "little" Catherine. He would meet up with his friends. He had their contact details and was going to let them know he would be visiting soon. The family decided on a summer holiday because of the sunny weather. Maria was excited. She had so much catching up to do with her cousin, Catherine. Cecilia bought two tickets for her parents on the Eurostar train to go visit Catherine in the summer of the following year. The train journey would take them through Paris and then London Waterloo. Catherine had got back from the USA where she had spent time with her extended family and was in a much better spirit. The crying had subsided, and she was beginning to accept her fate. Everyone she cared for so much seemed to be dying or was dead.

Brima was the only relative still in Giya village. His dad and mentor Alieu died several years ago. Almost all of Martha's children had passed away.

The war had ravaged the villages, towns and cities and the inhabitants had either been murdered in cold blood, raped, maimed, recruited into the rebel army or died of other illnesses. Some people left all their belongings and escaped the onslaught and went to big towns. Most of them went to Freetown. The city was overcrowded, and homelessness was increasing. There was no social housing, so many people slept wherever they could lay their heads at night. It became a twenty-four-hour buzzing city for the wrong reasons.

The country was also dealing with the Liberian refugee crisis, so it was challenging. Homeless people slept on street corners and dilapidated and burnt down buildings. Crime rates were on the increase because unemployment was high. The people from the villages were used to farming, but that was not feasible in the capital. The land space was not available. Development agencies like the Red Cross, World Food Programme, religious and non-religious-based organizations distributed food and clothing items to the displaced people and refugees. Schools were built and existing classrooms extended. Organizations provided books and educational packs for children. It was a chaotic environment, and it took time for subsequent governments to stabilize the situation. There was still room for improvement.

Brima had employed local boys to help him work on the farmland. They had a bad harvest that season due to destruction from the heavy rains. The bad weather has been a regular pattern due to climate change. The birds and bush rats also fed on the crops. The cassava field was badly damaged. The rats and squirrels had dug the soil around the plants to reach the cassava tuber. Three quarters of the crops were eaten. There was an infestation of rats. He had to do something about it. On a

171

market day, Brima went to get some rat traps and insecticides for the flies and mosquitoes.

He was determined to get his farm back to how it was before the war. A farm that produced decent crops free from pestilence. On a hot sunny day while he was clearing the bushes and chopping down the trees, a sharp object got in his right eye. He did not think very much of it. By the time he finished work and was ready to go home, his eye had swollen up. He could feel it. In the morning, the eyeball had blood. Some of the arteries burst, hence the blood. It looked bad. Catherine sent him money to go see an optician in Bo town. When he went, they prescribed eye drops and some paracetamol. After a few weeks, the swelling went down, and the blood was no longer visible. He was still having problems. His vision was blurry in both eyes. He asked his workers if it was cloudy, and they replied that it was sunny. This went on for a while. He attributed it to the incident with the stick and was going to give it time to heal.

Many months passed, and his vision was deteriorating. It was like a dark cloud all the time. News reached Freetown that Brima was losing his sight. Catherine was informed about this. She paid someone to take him back to the eye hospital in Bo. When they got there, Brima dialled Catherine's phone number. It rang for some time and then stopped. She was in her front garden talking to her passing neighbours and had left her phone on the sofa in her flat. When she went in, she saw three missed calls from Brima.

Although Catherine was younger than Brima, he called her aunt because she was now the provider, and her status had changed. She quickly returned his call and he answered immediately. Brima said, "Aunt Catherine, we are here at the eye hospital in Bo, and would you like to talk to the optician?"

Catherine responded, "Yes please, give them the phone". The optician was a sixty-year-old man and sounded mean on the phone. He had been working in the hospital for forty years. He started as an apprentice and had three years' training at the hospital before qualifying to offer treatments to patients. The Bo eye hospital had a training department. "Hello sir, please can you tell me about Brima's eye condition?", Catherine asked. The optician responded, "Madam, we are doing our best to ensure the patients are treated well in this hospital. He will do some tests, including the visual field, and scan his eyes to see what was happening. The specialist will take a look at the back of the eye for wear and tear". The phone went off during the conversation. Brima's battery was dead.

The optician did a thorough vision test and concluded he had cataract and some early signs of glaucoma. Instead of treating the underlying condition, he was given a pair of glasses and was told to come back for a checkup in two years. Brima naively accepted and paid them for their services. His vision improved slightly with the glasses, but he had terrible headaches. He was discharged, and he took the long journey back to the village. He continued working on his farm with the help of his employees. When they worked on the land, they sang their favourite songs in Mende. In the evening, they all sat around the fireplace and drank palm wine and the local gin. He was comfortable with his life because that was all he knew. He missed his family and the old boozey Giya. The centre for village parties. The warmth had disappeared, and it was different. He was surrounded by people he met after the war. He felt lonely most nights. He was a strong old man now but still unmarried and had no children. Sometimes, he visited relatives in Bumpeh and Bo.

His eyes had worsened, and he could hardly see. The cataract and glaucoma had weakened his vision. His eyes were gradually deteriorating. The nearest eye specialist hospital was miles away in Serabu. He was not comfortable with the journey and kept making excuses not to go there. He had lost confidence in the way he was treated in Bo and did not want to go back to see them because his case was not treated seriously, or they lacked the skills needed to treat his condition. Catherine advised him to go there but he refused. He did not trust the system and had stayed partially blind. He did not work very much on the farm. Catherine supported him financially when she could reach him.

Catherine was feeling much stronger now. Her mobility was getting better. On the day Maria and Joe arrived in London, they got a taxi that took them to their hotel in the Elephant and Castle. After dropping off their luggage, they ordered a taxi at the reception desk to take them to central London as they wanted to go sightseeing before meeting with friends and family. It was a sunny day, although it rained in the early hours of the morning. The weather forecast was good for the rest of the week, bright and sunny. They stayed a couple of nights at the Castle hotel in Elephant.

Amira arranged for a taxi to pick them up from the hotel to go stay with them. She had arranged a welcome barbecue party for them, inviting Catherine's friends and relatives. They came in large numbers. Some people were in the sitting room, kitchen, and garden. The children were up in the television room watching their favourite movies. Catherine was already at the house immaculately dressed in an African lace gown with gold and black sandals. Her makeup was naturally applied. Her fingernails and toes were painted red, and the colour matched her red lipstick. She looked amazingly pretty. She moved around with a walking stick. When Joe and Maria arrived, they were met at the door by Amira and her husband. They ushered them into the sitting room where Catherine was waiting. She stood up immediately when she saw them. The three of them embraced tightly. Tears flowed down the two ladies' cheeks. Maria and Joe were still in shock considering how time had passed. The last time they set eyes on each other was at a police family event in Grafton. It was forty-plus years ago. For some weird reason, the petite seven-year-old girl in Bo came flashing back in Joe's mind.

Amira took their bags to the guest room next to where Catherine would spend the night. Amira's house had steps, so it was not suitable for Catherine. When Joe and Maria sat down, they were offered drinks and then a loud welcome note by the DJ, who was playing soft background music. He gave the microphone to Amira, who spoke briefly about her grandaunt and her husband. She said they were visiting from Germany and the party was in their honour. Everyone rushed in to greet them and shook their hands. Food and drinks were served. When it was time to dance, the DJ played a popular Mende song Catherine had carefully chosen. That was what they listened to when they were growing up. It was a popular sixty's song, so everyone got up and danced. They had a delightful time, and, in the evening, the other guests left. Two of Amira's friends stayed behind to help tidy up. She took them to their rooms on the first floor. It was close to the toilet for easy access. They freshened up and went to bed.

In the morning, Amira knocked at the door to check on their guests. She asked them, "Would you like coffee or tea with or without sugar?" Maria came to the door and whispered, "White coffee, no sugar for Joe and a green tea for me, please?" She went off and prepared them. She brought them on a medium-sized tray to the room and handed the tray to Maria. t breakfast, Catherine, Maria and Joe talked about life back in Sierra Leone. Things they discussed included Martha's death and the disappearance of John, Catherine's dad. Joe was about to talk about what happened many years ago in Bo, when his phone rang. It was Cecilia checking on them. "Dad, hope you are having a good time?" She continued, "Mum getting on with Catherine?" Joe replied, "Everyone was doing great. Amira had a party for us when we arrived. It was pleasant and attended by lots of Sierra Leoneans".

The next few days, Joe and Maria's friends visited them. They went to visit one of Joe's ex-colleagues and stayed two nights with them in Kent. When they got back to Amira's house, they went gift shopping with Catherine. They got on bus twelve to Oxford Circus and went to Catherine's favourite shop, John Lewis. It had lifts between floors, so it was easy for them to navigate. Maria wanted to buy branded makeup for Cecilia, and shirts for her husband. Joe bought school bags with the Union Jack on them. They bought two white t-shirts with London printed on the front as a souvenir. They spent two weeks in London and went back to Germany. Catherine gave them a suitcase packed full of various clothing items for everyone.

Chapter 32 - Life Must Go On

Catherine, for many years, had wanted to go visit Sierra Leone. Her immigration status and health had restricted her from travelling overseas. She missed her relatives, friends, the culture, and the gossip. She had planned to visit Freetown and Bumpeh soon. The roads to Giya were still bad. They are only really for pedestrians, as four wheeled transport cannot use the narrow path, and it would be difficult for Catherine to walk the five to six-mile journey. In Freetown, she would need a car with a driver to travel around because of her injury. Among her siblings, she was the only surviving child and was grateful. Her thirteen siblings had all died from various illnesses, mostly brain aneurysms and strokes.

Her dad, John, disappeared from the face of the earth when he heard his teenage daughter was pregnant. He got very angry when someone crossed the line. To avoid problems, he went on a long journey and never returned to his family. The late Abdulai, Catherine's first husband, died during the rebel war. Her mum, Martha, passed away unexpectedly in the village with a suspected brain haemorrhage. Marian, her elder sister also died from an aneurysm, Caroline, her twin sister, died of breast cancer, and her husband, Leroy, died from cancer and other medical complications. Abbie and her husband died of natural causes.

Catherine woke up one morning and took the bus to Amira's house. When she arrived, Amira had gone to work. It was meant to be her day off. There had been a burglary at her new business. Thieves broke in during the early hours of the morning and stole equipment and products worth over three thousand pounds. Catherine had keys to the house, so she let herself in. When she got in, she went to the kitchen, filled the kettle with water from the tap and switched it on. She made herself a cup of mint tea and opened the biscuits and cookies container and put two crackers on the plate and spread margarine and soft cheese on the biscuits.

She sat down on the soft leather sofa and enjoyed her tea. The phone rang, it was Amira. "Hello mum, where are you? I have been trying to reach you all morning to let you know I had to leave home early this morning to attend to some urgent business matters". "Are you alright, mum?" Catherine responded, "I'm alright darling. The volume on my phone was low. I did not hear my phone ring. It had been playing up recently. I came to see you this morning, but you had already left. I'm still here". "What was the matter with your business?" "Nothing to worry about, just a small break in. The police forensic team had just left. They couldn't help. The thieves left no trace. It was well planned and carefully executed. They smashed the glass front door with a rock they brought with them and went in. We checked the security camera, and the thief was fully clothed with a balaclava and gloves". "He was seen dragging a huge bag out of the building and heading towards St George's Circus".

Catherine was startled. The plate of biscuits fell off her hand onto the floor. She was speechless and the sudden silence made Amira worry. She asked worryingly, "Mum, mum, are you alright?" Catherine said, "Yes, I'm fine, I was shocked. I know how hard you have worked and spent all your savings expanding your business. These days some people wait to destroy others' hard work and efforts." She remarked that nothing good would come out of the things they had stolen. She was furious. After speculation by the team, it was believed that someone familiar with the business had orchestrated the thieving. They knew where the products and equipment were. Catherine went back to her home after talking to her daughter.

Amira visited Catherine in the evening, and they discussed plans to visit Sierra Leone. Because it was her first trip back to Sierra Leone since she left and since she recovered from her illness, they both agreed that Amira would travel with her. The next day, Amira called the agency to enquire about dates and costs. When she called, a powerful male voice responded, Afrique agency, how may I help? Amira, "I would like two return tickets to Freetown from London, mid-December, coming back the first week in January for two adults. I need a wheelchair for my mum." "Alright, I will look," he responded. The agent did a search on his computer and came up with various dates. They decided on a date and time. Amira paid for the tickets with her credit card and received an email confirmation.

They wanted to escape the cold winter month to experience warm Christmas weather with relatives and friends. Christmas was different in Sierra Leone. It was always a joyous occasion with plenty and varieties to eat, drink and dance. The blasting of loud music could be heard five miles down the road. The children would look very pretty dressed up in their colourful clothes, socks and decent pairs of shoes. It was time to visit every family member and partake of their food and drinks. In small towns and villages there would be communal parties. The President would distribute gifts to households in his neighbourhood.

In the morning of the trip, Amira phoned her mum. She asked, "Are you ready? The taxi will be arriving in thirty minutes to pick you up". Catherine had been up since four am and was ready. She was so excited and had not bothered to eat breakfast. Amira arranged for the taxi to pick

179

her up before going to her mum's. When they got there, she was waiting in the parlour. She had pushed the two heavy cases to the door. The taxi driver helped lift the cases and put them in the back of the car. It was a medium size people's carrier. They all sat down and put on their seat belts. The driver drove through the narrow streets of Peckham through Croydon onto the main roads without any difficulties. It was very early in the morning and the roads were empty apart from a few buses carrying passengers to work. The journey to Gatwick took forty minutes.

When they arrived at the airport departure parking, Amira paid the fare and they both thanked him. He wished them a safe flight. Amira put the cases on a trolley while Catherine walked slowly with her walking stick beside her. Immigration and baggage checks went smoothly. The officer at the desk directed them to wheelchair assistance service. When they arrived, there was a long queue, so they waited for their turn. Catherine sat on the cold metal seats while Amira stood in the queue. When it was her turn, she said to the lady at the counter, "I booked a wheelchair for my mum. Her name is Catherine." The lady who was busy looking at a list of names on a sheet of paper, looked up and said, "Sorry, hello, how may I help?" She did not hear a single word Amira had just said to her, so she repeated what she had earlier said. "Oh yes, Catherine, she is on the list. Where is your mum?", she asked. Amira pointed at Catherine, who was looking at them. She waved her right hand. Ok, in just five minutes, someone will come to get her. They waited for eight minutes before a nice-looking lady came in with an empty wheelchair. The reception lady announced, "Wheelchair ready for Catherine." She got up with the aid of Amira and her stick as she was feeling stiff that morning. They breezed through immigration and then got on the shuttle to terminal C. They waited for an hour before boarding the plane.

On the plane, Catherine was given an aisle seat with a bit of leg room. Amira sat next to her. She was going back to her mother's land. They watched inflight movies and chatted as the plane flew through the clouds and bright sky. Amira was also following the flight paths. When they flew over the Atlantic Ocean, a firm but distinct voice came through the PA system. "It is your pilot here. All flight attendants ensured everyone was seated with seatbelts on. It's very windy so we are going to experience some turbulence." By the time he finished announcing, the plane dropped so badly, and the lights went out briefly. There was complete silence, one could hear a pin drop. Amira looked at her mum and they closed their eyes tightly and murmured some words of prayers.

After a few minutes the plane was stable again. The passengers were all thinking the worst was over, then it went into another set of turbulence. Everyone was concerned, there was a flight attendant, sitting in the corner next to the emergency door and was very anxious. He tried to disguise it, but it was obvious. People were looking around for the nearest emergency exit doors. It went on for a little while and then the pilot announced, "We have gone through the bad weather so from now on we are going to be fine". Everyone clapped. When they arrived in Conakry, Guinea, some passengers disembarked, and a new lot came on board. A flight attendant announced, "We are going to be here for sixty minutes to refuel before flying to Freetown, our destination. We wish to apologise for any delay". The plane was meant to be there for thirty minutes.

The journey to Lungi took thirty minutes. At the airport, the wheelchair personnel were waiting for

181

Catherine and all the other physically disabled passengers at the bottom of the steps. It was not a wheelchair friendly airport at the time. Two airport staff went on board to help her down the steps. Amira walked slowly behind them carrying the handbags. She was exhausted from the humidity and the long travel time. They had been up for more than twelve hours. The immigration process was straightforward with the officers welcoming them. Catherine was immediately recognised by an officer. He stood up and said aunty Catherine, "wow, why are you in a wheelchair? Do you remember me? My name is Lansana, and I worked with you at the shipping port many years ago as an apprentice".

He told his colleagues that Catherine was a very good person. She smiled and said, "Yes, your dad is Mr Kaisamba. You had left school and were learning the trade when the war broke out. How's your dad doing?" Lansana's face was a bit pale. "Dad and mum did not survive the war. They were both killed by the rebels". Catherine was shocked and sad by the revelation. She took his number and promised to give him a call. She told him that she had a terrible stroke that left her paralysed. She was returning home for the first time after the war.

The suitcases were collected from baggage control, and they went to look for Amira's friend, Isaac and the driver that were waiting for them. They had come to pick them up in a Landcruiser. They had missed the ferry, and the next one was in five hours. Also, Catherine was not too comfortable with the ferry crossing. It was always overcrowded and no real health and safety onboard. The drive home was exciting initially. They spoke about everything from politics, the economy, development to name a few. Amira's friend worked for a non-governmental organization. It was hot and humid, so the two ladies were sweating profusely. As they embarked on the dark and dusty roads, they heard two loud noises, and the vehicle was wobbly and slowed down. Amira exclaimed, "Stop, stop, the tyres!" The driver stopped immediately and got his torch out. There were no streetlights. The two men got out of the vehicle to check, and Amira was about to join them when Isaac said, "Please get back in, this place is not safe". They were in the middle of a deserted road where it had been alleged that thieves had robbed passersby. The next village was two miles away. They were surrounded by thick forests. The faulty tyres were replaced quickly with the spares that were in the boot of the vehicle. Those were the only spare tyres, so they had to be very cautious.

Catherine thought the roads from the airport to Port Loko had been upgraded after the war. When they reached the next village, the driver asked, "Would you like to use the toilets before we continue?" He had acquaintances in the village. His fiancée's parents lived in the tiny mud hut on the outskirts of the village. She was there visiting her parents, and they had arranged to meet on his way from the airport. When they stopped in front of the hut, she came out to greet them. She offered food to Catherine, Amira and Isaac, but they turned down the offer. They thanked her. The driver went in to greet his in-laws. On his way out, he whispered something in her ears and then kissed her on the forehead before handing over some cash from his pocket to her. He walked away and joined the others in the vehicle. "I'm so sorry for keeping you waiting. It's the right thing to do to stop and show respect to in-laws", he explained. He drove carefully through the village and exited on the lit main road.

They had arrived in Freetown. The streetlights were shining so bright. The roads had been resurfaced and marked distinctly. The city was built up and when they arrived in Kissy around the shell gas station, the streets were buzzing and the people bustling. The street hawkers were busy forcing their trade on the passing cars and passengers. Catherine was amazed and she was so moved, tears of joy rushed down her face. She was thinking that if she had died many years ago from an aneurysm, she would not have had the opportunity to go back to her beloved country. She chuckled, no place like home.

When they arrived at their destination in Aberdeen village, where Amira's daughter, Zee had rented a two-bedroom house close to the beach, they were met by her. She had recently moved back home to pursue a career in government. The driver took out the cases to the room Zee had prepared for them. She greeted them, "Hello mum, Hello grandma, welcome to Freetown. Hope you had a great trip!" She offered them water. What would you like to eat after you've freshened up. Let me show you around the house. When done, Amira and Catherine unpacked their cases, went to the bathroom and then sat down for dinner. Zee had cooked them various dishes; potatoes leaves, chicken stew, couscous and rice. They ate ravenously sat around the round table. Catherine was surprised Zee cooked those delicious meals.

After eating, they thanked her and went to sit in the veranda for some fresh air. As they sat down, they were greeted by the buzz of mosquitoes. Catherine had sprayed her hands and feet with the mosquito repellent but that did not stop them. They were bitten so badly. In the morning, there were patches of swollen skin on the arms and legs. Before travelling, they had gone to the travel centre in Victoria to get the required vaccines and medication for the trip and they were taking the tablets religiously because they knew what malaria meant.

In the morning, around six am, two of Catherine's nephews arrived and knocked frantically on the door. They had travelled from the other side of the city, from the hills of Wellington to get to Aberdeen. Who is that, asked Zee? She checked the entrance camera and saw the two desperate looking men. One of them responded, "It's Salieu and Manuel, we are here to see Aunt Catherine". She had told one of her relatives that she was coming to Freetown and the news had spread like wildfire. Zee, without opening the door said, "She is sleeping, please can you wait for me to wake her up!" Please make yourselves comfortable on the seats in the veranda. They were upset because she had not let them in the house. It was too early for someone to come visit.

Meanwhile, Catherine had woken up and was walking slowly with her walking stick towards the door. She enquired, "Who is that?" Zee responded, "Oh your nephews. They have come this morning to see you. How disgusting and selfish." They hadn't given you time to rest properly. Catherine opened the door, and invited them in. They embraced and expressed excitement at seeing their aunt. Salieu commented, "You have not aged at all, aunt. What is your secret?" She smiled and asked them, "Why have you come so early?" "We wanted to avoid the traffic. Sometimes the one-hour journey would take five or more hours due to the horrendous traffic in the city."

Catherine called Amira and asked her to offer the guests some coffee. Amira was tired because she had not slept all night due to the mosquitoes. Although they sprayed the room to repel them, for some reason, the insects had found their way into the room and were excited about their new arrivals. It's like the mosquitoes had sensed their un-bitten skin so they went for it with a vengeance. Amira was about to boil the kettle when Zee's domestic staff arrived and took over. She went to the kitchen and prepared the family breakfast and laid the table. The guests ate bread and boiled eggs with a cup of white coffee. They ate quickly because they were hungry and tired. The two men were served first while the ladies took showers and dressed up appropriately. When Catherine, Amira and Zee sat down to eat, another set of family members arrived. A family of five; two adults and their three children. Catherine's nephew, Abraham and family. He was the elder son of Catherine's twin sister, Caroline, who died of breast cancer. The food was not enough to go around so they shared with the three children and offered the parents coffee with milk.

After breakfast, Amira and Zee went into town to get some leones. They went to the commercial bank foreign exchange desk where Amira changed five hundred pounds to leones. Zee asked her mum, "what else would you like to do while we are in town?" "We can go to the market to get some food stuff and to the shops to buy groceries for the house", Amira replied. The drive into town was tiring and exhausting. The sunny weather and the horrendous traffic made it difficult to travel anywhere. Zee took her mum to her work place to meet her boss and colleagues. It was in the western area, Brookfields, in a tall government building. The office space was clean and modern. The air conditioner was blowing cold air, so it was a pleasant change. "Mum, come meet my boss?" Surprisingly, Amira knew Zee's boss. They grew up in the same area. She exclaimed with excitement, "What a small world!" "How are you doing? Zee is my daughter." "Really?", he enquired with his mouth wide open. "My word, what a small world. You have such a beautiful and talented daughter! She told us that her mum and grandma were visiting from London. Wow, I haven't seen you since secondary school. Should I tell your daughter that you were troublesome?" he said jokingly. Amira laughed out loudly and looked around the office, all eyes were on them, so she apologised for being a nuisance. "Well, she knows already," she continued.

They went around the office and greeted her colleagues and then left. Mum, "You seem to know everyone in the country." Zee complimented her mum. "You should have gone into politics or be some public figure." Amira was friendly and outgoing, when she was growing up in Freetown. She was one of the people who were the last to leave the dance floor. She was also a bright young girl but very playful. She wanted to be accepted by everyone she came across. She made good and bad friends. She was always in trouble in school and in detention some of the time. She had taken the traits of her mum, Catherine. Zee was the opposite of her mum; calm and calculating. But occasionally she would get very annoyed over a perceived affront or slight. When she was angry, no one could calm her down. Fortunately, that did not occur often.

When they finally got home, the house was in a state of chaos. The guest's children were running and jumping on the sofa and beds. The toilet roll was torn into pieces and littered all over the house. The television screen had been smashed by one of the children throwing a bottle at it. Catherine was on the veranda with the adults, so she did not know what was going on inside. They thought the children were watching television. Catherine's relatives were full of complaints; life had been difficult for them and that Amira and Precious had refused to support them financially. It was all about them saying negative and selfish things. Catherine let them finish ranting and then sighed. She looked at them with disdain. These were the people she worked so hard in London to support.

Sometimes she could not afford proper food and clothing.

She addressed them individually, telling them about their flaws and greed. She looked at them in their eyes and shook her head then, an outburst, "I was expecting you, my relatives to ask me about my health, my condition, my illness. How had I survived? I was pronounced dead but resuscitated and given a second chance to be able to come back to see all of you. Even in my sick bed, you kept asking for money and I fought with myself, my children to stop sending money but for the humanity in me, I always did. You make me sick!" she exclaimed. "What did you do with the money I sent you, she asked her late Caroline's son and wife? You asked for help to start a business. I sent you money to finish constructing my house, but you destroyed the initial structure and squandered the money on alcohol and God knows what else." They were not expecting this and wanted to apologise but she told them to be quiet.

She turned to the others and said, "Do you think money grows on trees in London? I worked hard to support every one of you until my demise. Every day, I get phone calls, people asking for one thing another. There was always a story; if someone was not on death bed, the children's school fees had not been paid or they had not eaten for months. I understand it's difficult out here and everywhere. Just try to get yourselves out of your present condition." Catherine continued, "my children are tired. They work so hard to support themselves and their families. Back in London, no one gives you money if you don't work for it. You are all young and healthy, so I would advise you to go out there, hustle and strive like other people". They were speechless, hoping the ground would just open and swallow them. Catherine was exhausted, now in her seventies, these people were still expecting her to keep supporting them and their families all in the name of living overseas.

Zee was extremely angry when she got home. She called the domestic staff who was in the backyard washing clothes. "Where were you when these children messed up my house?" Their parents got up to help but Zee asked them to stay out of it. Please do not come in here. Just keep those children out of here". She was astounded when she saw the broken television. She went into a rage and shouted, "Idiots, who broke my television?" The children were amused and giggled among themselves. It was like a planned job. We will go there and destroy their house. It was like a call for attention. Zee's heart was beating so hard. She looked at them and they pointed at each other causing more confusion. She went into her bedroom and slammed the door shut. Catherine called the children and asked, "Why did you smash up the place?" It's going to cost money to fix the television. Their parents did not say a word. No reactions from them and not even an apology. They were enjoying it all. The children were badly brought up. The house was cleaned up and dinner prepared. Zee stayed in her room listening to calm music.

At that point, Catherine went in and brought the gifts she had kept for them. She had placed twenty pounds each for all her nieces and nephews in brown envelopes. There were about twenty of them. She had carefully written their names on the envelopes. She also brought clothing items such as shirts, trousers, dresses, shoes and bags. She handed over their gifts. They served them dinner before they left. In the morning, Zee called the local technical engineer to check the television set. After having a look, he said, "It was still working for now, but you need to change the screen or buy a new one in future". The price of a new screen and installation fee was huge. After several months, she bought a new television set.

The following days and weeks saw a stream of relatives coming and going. Everyone of them coming to collect gifts, complained about the economy, their circumstances, and the fact that Amira and Precious were not helping them. It was like these people thought that living in foreign countries was that easy. Catherine told them that it was by grace, some people were still alive. She mentioned a few cases of people in prison, those affected by immigration and the increase in mental and physical illness. Unfortunately, these people only think about themselves. If they could ask Catherine to support them in her present condition, they would not care as long as their needs are met.

On Sunday, Zee took them to Lumley beach for a picnic. It was a lovely sunny day. The beach was packed full of people. There were families having barbecues, music of varying kinds and genre and young boys and girls dancing. The younger children were building sandcastles with their friends. It was a beautiful atmosphere. The current was high, so no one was swimming. At the far end were a few fishing boats and canoes. The fishermen were throwing nets in the sea. A canoe boat capsized in the morning hours after hitting a rock by the bank of the river. The two men were rescued by a passing trawler. Amira sighted an empty space under a large coconut tree at the far end of the beach. They quickly occupied it and placed down the picnic basket and mats on the sandy beach. They brought a green beach chair for Catherine to sit on because she could not get down on the mat. They had their hats and sunglasses to protect them from the sun.

When they sat down, they recognised several people they knew many years ago when they lived in

Freetown. There were also people from the US, Canada, Denmark, France and other countries on holiday. It was a joyous atmosphere. Catherine took her children to the beach when they were growing up. It was a Sunday treat. She picked up her walking stick and strolled along the riverbank. Amira went after her shouting. Mum, be careful. Don't go too close to the water. She waited for the water to come up to the sand so she could get her feet wet. She was a good swimmer, but the waves were strong, and she was a bit fragile. They ate roasted meat, pepper chicken and salads, drank ginger beer, water and danced to loud music. In the evening everyone packed up their things and went home.

The next day was a rainy day. They stayed home to watch the news and then settled down to popcorn and ice cream. At ten o'clock they went to bed. It was pouring down with heavy rains. At two in the morning, when they were sleeping, thieves came to the house. The two security officers that were meant to guard and protect them were sleeping. The thieves jumped over the iron gates, into the compound without them knowing. They were trying to open the window in Catherine and Amira's bedroom, when Amira woke up. She heard strange noises outside but thought it was the security guards talking. She switched on the light and to her surprise, two men pointed knives at her. They were trying to say something, but she could not hear it. With her loud voice, she shouted, "Thieves, thieves, thieves".

Everyone woke up and Zee switched on the main light. Suddenly, the light went out. It was a blackout. The main cable leading to the house had been destroyed. They got the giant touch out and lit it. The security guards immediately put on the generator. The thieves knew they had to run. They quickly jumped over the fence and disappeared into the darkness. In the morning, they looked around to see if everything was in place. Unfortunately, Amira's friend's car was parked outside that evening. She had borrowed the car to use it the following day to take Catherine to see her friends. The thieves broke in and stole the music player and removed the four tyres of the car. They mistakenly left the tools used for their operation. They were not relevant because no one was going to offer forensic. Amira asked the security guards if they did not hear or see the thieves. These people were professional thieves. The security guards were useless. As soon as they were questioned, one of them ran away and never came back. The other guard who lived in the neighbourhood was sacked. They were replaced by a professional agency.

Chapter 33 – Return To London

At the end of the four weeks in Freetown, Catherine and Amira left for London. In the morning Zee drove them to the fast boat terminal to catch the speed boat to Lungi, the airport. She paid forty dollars each for the ride. Catherine struggled to get on board but when she did, she grabbed a life jack and put it on. All the passengers were given one. The luggage went in a different boat.

Amira asked the captain of the boat, a young man who was smartly dressed and had a distinctive life jacket on. "Hello young man, sorry if I may ask, what is your name and where did you learn how to captain a boat?" "How old are you?" He looked like a teenager. He smiled and said, "I'm happy you asked because I do get strange looks in this job. My boss taught me how to ride a boat. We had an hour on the sea and that was it. I was an apprentice for two years and was on the job for almost one year. I'm married with three children". Ok, that's not true. You're joking. Amira commented. The other passengers were amazed, and another repeated the same question, "how long have you captained this boat?" or something similar. Well, as I said earlier, "I have worked for this company for one year as a captain". He said, "We are about to leave now, if you have any further questions, please do not hesitate to ask, when we get to Lungi", he said sarcastically. He was very serious.

He asked his men to get the boat ready for departure and they left for the crossing. The ride was scary with the boat bouncing very hard on the water as they travelled across the bay. There were fishing boats and container ships all around the water. It was a skill to know what to do if there was an incident. After thirty minutes they arrived on the shores of Lungi. A coach with the luggage was waiting to take them to the airport.

At the airport, Amira went to get a trolley to put the luggage. They walked to the wheelchair service desk to request one. The lady who assisted Catherine, was young, cheerful, and very helpful. The immigration and bag check processes went smoothly. Catherine recognised some of the workers at the airport and that helped. They finally got on the plane and flew via Guinea Conakry. There was a delay of an hour there. The Conakry bound and transit passengers got off and new ones got onboard. The aircraft had to refuel before departure. The journey to London was straight forward. When they arrived at London Gatwick, the aircraft had to wait in a queue on the runway. It took about ten minutes to get to the arrival gate. The wheelchair assistants were already waiting. As soon as the doors were opened, all the other passengers had got off, then the assistants went onboard to help the physically challenged passengers.

Catherine sat on the wheelchair provided for her. They went through immigration and collected the cases. At the arrival lounge, the taxi driver was waiting for them. He had a placard with Amira's name on it. When they saw him, they walked up to him and introduced themselves. He led them to his car, which was parked in the car park on the first floor. They thanked the assistant as they got in the car. Catherine gave her a tip, but she refused to take it. She said, "Ma'am just doing my job". She rode away and the driver drove off. It was getting cold and windy in the UK. The driver, a West African man, asked, "how was your holiday?" Catherine said, 'I have had a good time in Freetown. It's great to be back. The weather was too humid, and those mosquitoes were annoying. I love my country, and I will go back next year but next time I will be better prepared." Amira nodded and said it was pleasant. They were not happy about the state of the country. There was development in parts but the constant begging and poverty in the city centre made them sad. The war had brought everyone to the city and the unemployment rate had soared. The roads had been upgraded but there was still a lot more to do. Electricity was ad hoc and water supply seemed scarce in some areas. The government was doing their best to improve the country.

Back in London, Catherine went back to her flat. It was freezing so she had a runny nose. Her friends had missed her, and they were waiting to welcome her. They cooked nice meals for her. She was popular and supportive in her community. She settled back in quickly and continued with her usual routine. On Sundays, she went to church.

One evening after her usual phone call with Amira, she fainted. Amira had suspected something very strange that evening. She kept dropping her phone on the floor. She asked, "Mum, are you alright?" She replied, "yes, I'm just tired". Ok, go to bed and I will give you a call in the morning. Amira did not think much of it. Some days Catherine got confused and because she did not sleep very well, she was always tired. In the morning, Amira took some food for her mum. She had cooked the previous night and stored it in a refrigerator. When she arrived at eight o'clock, the door was locked with the internal security chain in place. She found that strange. Normally, Catherine woke up at six am and went to an early morning prayer at a church across the road. She usually used the spare key to open the door but the security chain inside was always off the hook. This time it was securely fastened, and Amira could not get in.

She knocked at the door. "Mum, are you there? Please open the door?" With a very faint voice, Catherine responded that she was coming. That went on for five minutes. The voice was coming from the direction of the bathroom. Amira thought her mum was taking a shower. She waited for another five minutes and called again, "Are you in the bathroom?" The faint voice kept repeating the same thing. "I'm coming". The response was getting weaker. She could hardly hear what she was saying. Amira called the housing management team to inform them what was happening. After several attempts, someone came on and said, "I will inform the team. Someone will be with you as soon as they can".

Amira was worried and it was taking longer for help to come. She called 999 and requested an ambulance and fire service. "My mum is locked in her flat and I can't reach her. I think she is unwell", she told them. "Ok, madam, what's your mum's name and address?", the operator asked. "Catherine, Peckham, Southeast London, flat 9", Amira replied. After a couple of minutes, the operator said, "the fire service has been notified, they will help unlock the door. The paramedics have been contacted as well. Amira waited for ten minutes, and no one had come, she went out of the compound to seek help. She needed someone to help her unlock the chain so she could get to her mum to ascertain what was happening. A van was passing, she took off her shoes and ran after it shouting, 'help, help, help' and beckoning for the driver to stop. Raising her hands in frenzy like a mad lady. The driver saw her through his rear mirror and stopped briskly. He wound down his glass and asked curiously, "What's the matter lady? Are you alright?" Before he finished his asking, without hesitation, Amira lamented, "my mum is unwell, and I can't reach her. The door is locked. I need help to unscrew the security chain". I'm really worried about her."

The young man jumped out of his vehicle and assured her that he would do his best to open the door. He opened the back of the van and took out his toolbox and took out a screwdriver. He was a handyman. They ran fast to the door, and he started the task of unchaining the door. Luckily, he had a slim body and could easily slide his head and hand through the half open door to unscrew the nuts. There were many nuts and screws, so it took him several attempts to take them off. He struggled with unlocking one of the screws, so he ran to his van to get another screwdriver and plier.

When he got the door opened, Amira thanked him and ran into the bedroom where her mum laid down unconscious on the floor. "Mum, what's wrong?" Catherine had stopped responding and was breathing but could not get the words out. It was already forty minutes since Amira had been trying to get to her. She must have been unwell since the previous night. The van driver was with them before the fire service arrived but there was nothing for them to do. While they were checking on Catherine, the paramedics arrived. They asked, "are you related to the patient? What's her name and what really happened?" She explained the

197

course of events and that she had only reached her because the door was locked.

The paramedics, two men, asked everyone to stay in the sitting room as the bedroom was too small. They lifted Catherine gently on the bed and checked her blood pressure, airways, eyes, and ECG. She was very weak to walk, so they brought in a stretcher to put her on it. They took her to the ambulance to do further checks. They decided to take her to hospital. Amira went with them. In hospital, they did all the necessary tests and head scans. She was given IV fluid because she was dehydrated. She regained consciousness.

The results came back normal. She complained of pain in her entire body especially her numb leg. She emphasised the pain in her waist and left foot. She lamented, "it is excruciating doctor. The pain is too much". "It sounds like sciatica", the doctor commented. The doctor asked, "when did you start feeling the pain?" Catherine said, "my medication was reviewed several months ago, and the doctors made a decision to cut down on my pain killers because it was making me dizzy". The feeling of faintness and dizziness had started two years ago but were infrequent. The medical team went off to check her records and prescriptions on the system. It was obvious that taking away the strong pain inhibitors was causing the pain, but they did not know what was causing the fainting. The blood sugar was normal. They continued giving her a few more drips. She said, "I'm hungry". The nurse brought her a cup of tea with milk. Amira went to the shop to get a sandwich. Catherine drank the tea but refused to eat the bread. She said, "I have no appetite". She slept while Amira sat next to the bed on a grey armchair. They were later moved to the fragility ward to be monitored. The following day, she was discharged and that made Amira furious.

When she went to pick her up from hospital, they had already moved her mum to the vehicle waiting area. She has been there for more than three hours. She looked frail. Tears flowed down her cheeks as the two eyes met. "Why are you crying, mum?" She asked. "When I was in the ward, a nurse came in the morning and told me that I was going home. I don't feel very well", Catherine spoke in a sad tone. Amira embraced her mum and told her not to worry. "I will get to the bottom of it" Amira assured her just to comfort her. There wasn't much she could do anyway. She went to the nurses' desk and demanded to talk to her mum's doctor. "Oh madam, the doctors are all very busy attending to other patients. Please go talk to Catherine's general practitioner (GP)." "Very patronising," she thought. "My mum has been discharged without anyone talking to me," Amira continued. "Well, we can't help but please let me check her notes". She spent five minutes scrolling the screen and finally found her record and said there wasn't much to report on. They hadn't updated the record as yet. At the bottom of the note, she saw medication to be reviewed in six months. They had offered some more light painkillers. "She has been discharged from here," the nurse confirmed.

The drop off ambulance driver came to collect the patients. Catherine was prioritized because she was looking very fragile. He commented, "why is she going home?" He had seen Catherine brought in the previous day to A & E. He said, "I remember you two yesterday. Your mum was rushed in while we were waiting with our patients at reception. You looked very worried and when they took her in you were pacing around". They had seen them. "You care very much for your mum," he complimented. Amira smiled and said, "Well they don't know what was wrong with her. They had referred her to the GP."

The driver was very caring and helped his patient. He had a Jamaican accent. He secured Catherine in the far-right corner of the vehicle and asked Amira to sit next to her. The other patients sat in their seats and were strapped in well with the seatbelts. Catherine was closer to the hospital, so he dropped them at her house in Peckham. He helped take her in and ensured she was safe before leaving. When they were alone, Amira prepared vegetable soup for her mum and encouraged her to eat. She spent the night watching over her mum. She felt better after the soup and a big cup of tea with lots of milk. Catherine felt better for a couple of days and Amira decided to go back to work. She asked her mum's friends to watch over her. She was popular with her friends and neighbours. Her church friends were informed so they visited during the day.

One evening when she was eating dinner, she felt very dizzy. Amira was with her. She collapsed on the dining table. "Mum, mum, what's wrong? Are you ok?", Amira asked. No response from Catherine. She moved her to the nearest sofa and got a wet towel to wipe her face. She was sweating. Her clothes were wet like a bucket of water had been poured on her. Her body temperature was high. Amira called the ambulance service and later called Precious. She thought her mum was dying. Catherine started gasping for her breath. It was horrible and very scary. The wait for help took some time. Amira's husband had arrived to support her. Other family members came as they hear the news. Catherine murmured, "no hospital, no ambulance". Every time anyone mentioned hospital, she waved her hands with anger and dragged her words. She may have given up.

Amira called the ambulance service again. While she was on the phone, Catherine spoke faintly but frantically, no ambulance please. She refused to go to hospital and got agitated whenever, someone mentioned hospital. The operator must have heard her saying, no ambulance. The ambulance finally arrived, and the paramedics gave her oxygen to help with the breathing. They spent about twenty minutes assessing her. "Let's take her to hospital. I'm suspecting infection", said one of the paramedics. Catherine did not want to go. She was adamant. Her recent experience in hospital had frightened her. She hated been left on her own in a private room at night.

Amira went in and sat on the bed besides her. She said, "Mum, one last time please. I promise they are going to help this time. Don't you want to see your grand and great grandchildren grow up?" Catherine loved her family, and she would do anything to make them happy. She opened wide her eyes and nodded in agreement. They took her in a wheelchair to the ambulance and Amira went with them. They went to a different hospital as requested by Amira just for a change. The hospital was further away so they drove past the Elephant to get there. She was taken into the accident and emergency department. Some new tests were done, and they treated her with antibiotics. She stayed in hospital for one week and no one was allowed to visit her until the day she was discharged. The hospital had a strict policy on visiting patients in certain wards because of the risk of covid.

Catherine felt much better when she left hospital. She had a review after three months. They gave he a new medication for the pain. Amira moved in and stayed with her for three months. She could not get herself to sleep in her own house leaving her mum on her own at night. It was a difficult time for her. She closed her business most of the time to look after her mum. She prepared the meal and ensured that she was taking the correct doses of her medication. Catherine had been on seventeen medicines since the aneurysm. The doses had been

201

increased and decreased depending on how she was feeling. The pain killers were taken off when she started fainting and feeling dizzy. That led to the chronic waist and foot pain. The high doses had camouflaged the pain for many years.

One Saturday morning, Amira decided to carefully check her prescription and the medicines her mum was taking daily. To her surprise, she realized that she was overdosing on some of the medicines. She called the GP to let them know what she had discovered. The fainting was due to overdosing on her medication. Reflecting on the fainting episodes, it had always happened after taking the nights drugs. The GP instructed the pharmacy to sort out a medicine pack for her. That system was efficient, and she would only take the medication as required. The packaged were delivered weekly and sealed. The instructions on how to take them was boldly written on each container. Since the new system, Catherine had recovered from the dizziness and did not collapse for several years.

Chapter 34 - Trip To The USA

Precious and her children were missing Catherine and had not been able to be with her due to their heavy workloads. They lived in Philadelphia, in the US. It would take them ten or more hours to fly to London. Precious called one weekend and said, "mum, would you like to come and visit? The grandchildren will take it in turn to help look after you so Amira can get some rest and you can recuperate". "Yes, it's a great idea. Let me discuss it with your sister so she can buy the ticket and sort out insurance", Catherine replied. She was very excited about the idea of going to see her family. She called Amira to tell her about the trip. "Darling, your sister would like me to go for a couple of months so you could have some rest. What do you think", she asked. Catherine had already accepted the invitation without discussing it with Amira. She had been cautious not to sound ungrateful. She realised that Amira needed some rest and for her to concentrate on her business. They had a family virtual meeting to discuss the logistics and finance. Amira was concerned about the long flight and that Catherine was going to fly on her own. The ticket was bought, and the huge insurance cover paid for the trip.

In the morning of the trip to the states, Catherine woke up very early in the morning around six o'clock. The flight was scheduled to leave at eleven forty-five. Amira had ordered a taxi the previous night. The driver arrived and Amira was already at her mum's house waiting. The drive to the airport was quick. It was early in the morning and the streets were quiet. At the airport. Amira got a trolley for the luggage, and they went to the flight desk to check in. The lady at the check-in desk asked, "who is travelling?", Catherine responded, "It's me". She handed her passport to the lady and Amira lifted the luggage and put on the weighing scale. Everything was fine. She gave Catherine her boarding pass and wished her a safe flight.

At the wheelchair service desk, Amira explained her mum's condition to the staff and asked the personnel to be careful and make sure she got on the flight. She thanked her before they went through immigration. She hugged, kissed her mum and said, "safe trip and call me when you get there, ma. A wheelchair will be ready when you arrive." Tears filled her eyes, Catherine patted her daughter's back and said, "see you soon". She turned to the staff, "my mum is not strong so please take good care of her until she boards the plane. Any problem, this is my number". Amira handed over a piece of pre-written sheet with her name and telephone number on it. The lady nodded and smiled. As they disappeared amongst the crowded passengers, it dawned on Amira that her beloved mum was going away for a while. She knew her sister, Precious and her children would be gentle and kind to Catherine. They lived in the same house in Freetown and had suffered as a unit during the war in Sierra Leone. Catherine had been the mum and grand mum the children loved and trusted.

Various activities had been planned for her. She would go to the gym classes and water exercises to strengthen her core. There was the swimming and hot bath pool she liked so much. They had it all laid down for her. It was a well-being vacation. When she arrived at the airport, Precious and the children were waiting patiently for her. She had only seen her mum twice since the aneurysm, so it was high time, and they were looking forward very much to her visit. They drove home where the great grandchildren and other family members were waiting to welcome her.

As they were about to enter the house, the light came on and the children shouted, "surprise! Welcome granny". The house had been decorated with balloons and colourful decorations. There was a welcome banner on the wall facing the door. The children ran to her and hugged her. She felt at home. They took her to her bedroom and helped her in the bathroom to freshen up. She dressed up in a beautiful black and silver dress and went downstair join the guests. Dinner was served and then there was music and some dancing. Catherine was a bit tired, so she went to bed a bit early leaving her guests to continue the party.

In the morning, Catherine woke up, had a wash, and went back to bed. Precious was in the kitchen preparing breakfast for the family. She took some to her mum's room to serve her in bed. She had made pancakes and decorated them with strawberries, blueberries, pineapples, and syrup. "Mum, tea or coffee?" she asked. "Tea, milk no sugar please", Catherine replied. Alright, will be back with your tea, she said. She took her a cup of tea with milk. After eating, Amira took the dirty plates and cutlery to the kitchen and washed them. She thanked her daughter for a delicious meal. The great grandchildren woke up and went into Catherine's room. "Good morning grandma, hope you slept well? Yes, I had a great night. I slept like a baby, thanks." She responded. The children jumped in and laid down on the bed. She was meeting two of her great grandchildren for the first time. She was delighted. She had six in numbers and five grandchildren. In the afternoon, they went to the park and the children played on the slides and swings. The boys went on their roller skates while the older children walked with their grandma. Later in the day, they stopped for lunch at a nearby Mexican restaurant.

The next day, Precious' eldest daughter, Princess took Catherine to the gym. The gym was an hour away. It was a multi-complex building with many wellness facilities. They had a beautiful running track, steam room, sauna, swimming pools, hot baths and many more. They had professional classes for all ages. She had been signed up to chair and water yoga to help build her muscles and mobility. Some days she would be there for two hours. After two weeks, Catherine was physically and mentally fit and could walk without her walking stick. She enjoyed the drive every morning to the gym.

One Saturday afternoon, there was a carnival in town. They drove to the waterfront where the event was taking place. It was packed with people when they arrived. There were live bands, food stalls, carnival participants and it was buzzing with people. It was a pleasant atmosphere. The families had a wonderful time. At home, the grandchildren sat with their grandma, and she told them stories about growing up in the village of Giya. The children liked old tales and parables she told them. It was school holiday, so they were allowed to stay up late into the night with the family all gathered around the large marble floor seating room. The light from the sky shone through the lace curtains in the house. They watched the stars and moon. It was a delightful time for the family.

She was full of sadness when her holiday was coming to an end. On the day of her return to London, Precious rented a big van and they seated everyone to the airport. It was an hour drive to the airport. It was emotional and tears came running down their faces when they said goodbye to her. They formed a circle at the airport with Catherine in the centre. Precious and her family walked up and hugged her and gave her a kiss on her forehead and cheek.

Chapter 35 - Back In London

When Catherine arrived in London, she was met by Amira and husband. She was re-energised and looked well. Her mobility had improved, and she walked without her walking stick. The first six months was amazing, then on a fateful afternoon, as she was walking down the busy street of Peckham rye after a grocery shopping with her daughter, she tripped and fell on the hard pavement. "Are you alright?" Amira asked. She was alarmed and threw the shopping bags in the air to rescue her mum, but it was too late as she was already on the floor and unable to get up.

Before they left the house, Amira had encouraged her mum to use the walking aid which she carried on that day. Amira exclaimed, "help. Please can somebody help?" Two men rushed to the scene and helped lift her up from the dirty ground. Catherine was humiliated. Her self-esteem tumbled. She cried as she looked vulnerable and fragile. It had happened in front of a food store frequented by people she knew from Sierra Leone and her church. One of the men enquired, "Is your mum alright?'

Amira replied, "yes, she tripped on the loose pavements. It's a small fall and she should be fine." Amira helped her mum as they walked slowly to her place, which was around the corner not too far from where the incident had occurred. At home, Amira checked her mum's body for bruises. She sustained a small cut on her knee. Later in the evening, she complained of pain in her hip and left leg. She had refused to go to the hospital, so her daughter applied some ointment and gave her a massage. She then settled down in bed.

In the morning, her daughter phoned Catherine to check on her. "Hello mum, how are feeling now? Hope you slept well?" She replied, "yes darling, not too bad. I feel some pain in my leg. I would like to join the spa in Dulwich so I can go swimming." "What about Peckham pulse which is closer", Amira asked. She replied, "Peckham Pulse was being renovated at the moment. Please can you take me there any time this week?" Amira said, "OK, mum, I will come at eight am and we can get the bus there." Thank you, dear, she replied. In the morning, Amira went to her mum's place. She was still in bed. It was unusual for Catherine to be in bed at that time of the morning. She rushed in and asked, "why are you still in bed? What's wrong?" She could not move her left leg. Amira asked her to get up, but she cried out, "Pain". The pain was excruciating. She could barely move. "OK, mum, you go back to bed. She went to the medicine cabinet and brought out some painkillers and water and gave them to Catherine.

She went to the kitchen and cooked a small pot of oatmeal porridge and added milk to it. She toasted a slice of bread and spread margarine and cheese and took it to her bedroom. She helped her mum to the bathroom and assisted her wash and brushed her teeth. She helped dry her body with the towel, then massaged some lavender oil on the affected area. Mum, "the food is for you", pointing at the tray with the food. "I'm not hungry" Catherine stammered her words. "OK mum, just eat something so you can feel better. You need to take your medication, but I won't give them to you until you eat something. She finally got up reluctantly and took a spoonful and then wiped her mouth and laid down in bed. She was depressed and looked away. Frustrated about her condition, she reminisced about her youth; her good old days, she called it. She was grateful for those days.

Amira took her to see the doctor. He recommended a scan and a referral to adult social services. On the day of the scan, Catherine and Amira took a taxi to the main hospital. They arrived an hour before the appointment. The wait was long and when it was her turn, the exercise took less than ten minutes. The specialist said the result would be sent to her doctor, who would convey it to her. A week after the scan, Catherine received a letter. It read, your scan result did not show any broken bones or fractures. There was inflammation around the patella, around your knee. I have prescribed something to help reduce the swelling. "Go to the pharmacy and get your medication". Amira went to the pharmacy to collect the drugs and gave some to Catherine as instructed. She encouraged her to drink plenty of water.

After a week, she felt better, and continued with her daily routine. Her friends were visiting and bring food for her. She was popular among her family and friends. Her new neighbours were also friendly, and they spent the evenings chatting and playing dominos. She had inherited the set from her late husband. When he was alive, they would go to the main hall and compete with other occupants. She was always winning. She had played it for years. It always brought smiles to her face and took away the pain. She said after one of her games, "this brings me joy whenever I win a game." She was the queen's mother loved by everyone.

Catherine was well-known in Peckham and the southeast of London. Her nieces and nephews would visit from time to time. Despite her disability, she went to see friends and relatives in hospitals. She cared for older and more vulnerable people in her community. In the evening, the group of tenants would meet in the hall. The men gathered in the tenant's room to watch television, play games, drink rum or juices. The ladies baked chocolate and carrot cakes for the games' nights. One evening, as Catherine walked into the hall, the chairman of the association got up and announced, "ladies and gentlemen, tonight is going to be a special night. We have an award ceremony. The executive of the housing association had discreetly organised some pleasantries. Secret ballots have taken place, and the winners had been selected." Catherine won the award as the all-rounder. They partied all evening.

She was overwhelmed and proud to be recognised. The following day some of her friends brought her flowers and continued the celebration in her flat. They played dominoes and nibbled on leftovers from the previous day.

Printed in Great Britain
by Amazon